Hybrid Creatures

Yellow Shoe Fiction
Michael Griffith, Series Editor

</ hybrid creatures/>

{ STORIES }

Matthew Baker

Louisiana State University Press

Baton Rouge

Published by Louisiana State University Press
Copyright © 2018 by Matthew Baker
All rights reserved
Manufactured in the United States of America
First printing

Designer: Laura Roubique Gleason
Typefaces: Minion Pro and Corbel (text), Chaparral Pro (display)
Printer and binder: Sheridan Books

"Coder" originally appeared in *New England Review* in 2015 under the title
"Sensei"; "The Golden Mean" originally appeared in *The Missouri Review*
in 2015; "Movements" originally appeared in *The Southern Review* in 2016.

Library of Congress Cataloging-in-Publication Data
Names: Baker, Matthew (Children's story writer), author.
Title: Hybrid creatures : stories / Matthew Baker.
Description: Baton Rouge : Louisiana State University Press, [2018] | Series:
    Yellow Shoe Fiction
Identifiers: LCCN 2017037224 | ISBN 978-0-8071-6886-8 (pbk. : alk. paper)
    | ISBN 978-0-8071-6887-5 (epub) | ISBN 978-0-8071-6888-2 (pdf)
Classification: LCC PS3602.A58664 A6 2018 | DDC 813/.6—dc23
LC record available at https://lccn.loc.gov/2017037224

The paper in this book meets the guidelines for permanence and durabil-
ity of the Committee on Production Guidelines for Book Longevity of the
Council on Library Resources. ⊚

Contents

Coder

1

The Golden Mean

26

Movements

41

Proof of the Century

70

Acknowledgments

125

Hybrid Creatures

Coder

\<html\>
In the morning, on the way to campus, I stopped by the building where sensei lived. The tabby cat, a local stray, was sunning in the alley between the pawnshop and the pharmacy. It greeted me with a yawn, stretched, blinked, stood, inspected a clump of weeds, and then slunk off toward the dumpster.

I let myself inside the building with the keys sensei had given me. I collected the mail from his mailbox—junk mail, an operation that sensei said seemed almost quaint in the era of spam mail—then climbed the stairs to his apartment. The rooms were quiet. The furniture, the curtains, everything was exactly the same as yesterday. He wasn't here, and hadn't been.

For five weeks, sensei had been missing. Missing from the material world—his apartment—and, especially concerning, from the immaterial world—the internet. Five weeks before, he had promised to teach me a "legendary, very rare technique, invented by hackers in Utah," but then had vanished the next day. He had left his phone on the toilet, his jacket on the futon, the lamps lit, the shower running. Unusual, obviously. In the time since, he hadn't posted, tweeted, blogged anything. His email accounts hadn't been accessed once. If he had been arrested, wouldn't the news have said?

Today, like every day, I put on a record, a classical album, selected randomly from the shelf above the futon. Classical, that was all that sensei had. Warbling voices, in foreign languages, with gongs crashing in the background. I didn't mind. At soft volume, that kind of thing could be the perfect soundtrack for doing chores. I rolled up the legs of my jeans, pushed up the arms of my sweatshirt, and got to work. I swept the tiled floor in the kitchen, dusted the cupboard in the hallway, adjusted the radiator in the bathroom, and watered the herbs growing in ceramic pots on the windowsill in the bedroom. That was that. With sensei missing, there were no dishes to scrub and rack, no bags of trash to haul down to the alley below. I wasn't even sweating.

I cracked the windows to let in some fresh air, then heated water in the kettle. Outside, the gutters were streaming with thawing snow—on the wind, there was the smell of wet bark, damp paint, wet soil, damp brick. Taxis honked at taxis. Seagulls wheeled around a water tower. As soon as the kettle began rumbling ("not too hot, for sencha, or the tea will turn bitter!") I steeped a pot of tea and then sat on the futon, in a patch of wavering sunlight, staring at the door, wishing sensei would come bursting through. I really missed sensei. I sipped, and stared, and sipped, and stared.

Structurally, the source code for every webpage had exactly two elements: the head and the body. Viewing a webpage in your browser, you didn't see what was in the head. The head, that data in there, wasn't displayable. Only the body was. But, still, no webpage was a body only.

What was in my head just then? What jumble of thought and feeling?

<head> curiosity theories anxiety worries </head>

Where had sensei gone? Why had he taken neither phone nor jacket? Was he dead, imprisoned, sick, hiding from government authorities in an underground bunker? Was he somehow testing me?

I hacked but wasn't yet a hacker. I was an apprentice. I did chores in exchange for lessons. I wouldn't be a hacker until sensei said so.

Was the apartment being watched?

I was dying to learn that new technique.

Outside, in the alley, the tabby was mewing. Hungry for breakfast. The chef was late. I washed the teacup, emptied the strainer, rinsed the teapot, latched the windows. In the kitchen, the window was cloudy, spotted with dried raindrops, would need cleaning tomorrow. From my angle as I buttoned my coat, the windowpane displayed me, a faint reflection.

<body> buzzcut forehead eyebrows eyelashes eyes birthmark nostrils crossbite jaw </body>

Then I knelt for my backpack, and the windowpane displayed only city.

Somebody had been smoking in the stairwell. The stoplight was signaling go to an empty street. I bought a can of tuna from the bodega at the corner, peeled back the lid, and set the can in the alley, where the tabby was waiting. It sniffed at the tuna, then turned away to examine a pebble, pretending not to want to eat. Today, like every day, it would wait until I was gone.

</html>

<html>

By the time I got to campus, my history class had already started. I peeked through the door—the window was embedded with a mesh web to prevent the glass from being broken—and saw the professor lecturing at the chalkboard, gesturing at the map drawn there, ambiguous territories with smudged borders. The policy was, a tardy counted as an absence. We had been instructed, if we were late, not to come at all.

My grade would get lowered automatically. Still, having to ditch the lecture wasn't all bad. I really didn't like to hear about things like aqueducts and buttresses anyway. Plus, this meant that I could spend some time practicing hacking techniques, and could visit the teaista.

My face was still pressed against the window. A kid chewing tobacco, spitting into an empty soda bottle, was glaring at me from the back row. I tightened the straps of my backpack, slipped out the building, and hurried across campus, heading for the teahouse.

I followed a number of people, but the teaista was my favorite. She worked at the teahouse—the morning shift, today. Wait, what did that mean, "followed"? When other people "followed" somebody, that usually meant subscribing to wall posts, blog feeds, shared images, music playlists. Browsing public content, the few published artifacts of a life. But when the apprentice of an internationally notorious hacker "followed" somebody, that usually meant something far more involved. Hacking private content, mining every last bit of biographical information. The teaista, for example. I read her emails—both inbox and outbox—monitored her bank accounts, watched her video chats, studied the poetry that she drafted and always deleted days later, unfinished. That was my "following." Stalking, technically. The stalking was nonsexual. She was, after sensei, the central figure in my life.

What was in her head just then?

<head> drowsiness memories
loneliness inventories </head>

Cramps had awoken her last night, intermittently. That and nightmares about morgues. Tomorrow was the anniversary of the date her mother had died, thirteen years ago, which also had been the date of her high school graduation. Lately the looming anniversary had left her dazed, overwhelmed by memories, visions of her mother doing commonplace activities: mopping, choosing a board game piece, rummaging through a purse to pay the fare for a bus. She had been trying to focus on work. She had been feeling distracted. As manager she had to keep inventory for the teahouse—how much flour, how many limes, how much anise, how many eggs remained before an order needed to be placed. She also kept inventory for herself, obsessively. She kept lists of manga she was "dying" to read. She kept lists of her shortcomings. She kept lists of appointments to make, prescriptions to fill, recipes to try, ideas for poems. She kept lists of signs that she was aging. She had not had a date in years. To her roommate, she claimed she "never ever" wanted to get married. To her sister, who was married, she admitted she "desperately" wanted to find somebody, and was losing hope she ever would. She fell asleep clinging to pillows, pretending the lumps were a body.

The teahouse sat on a street of absolutely ordinary houses. Brick walkways, plastic trash barrels, bicycles chained to iron fences. A mangy dog sniffing a manhole cover. There was no sign to indicate that the teahouse was a business rather than a residence. Or were the other houses on this street also unidentified businesses? I had never tried any of the other doors.

The gate was open. Patches of shade from the maple trees were changing shape like clouds across the patio. I twisted the doorknob, stepped through the door.

Inside, an elderly couple sat murmuring at a weathered table with mismatched stools. Steam wisped from the rims of their teacups. Otherwise the tables were empty. The teahouse had an ambience of darkness: a ceiling of exposed wooden beams, walls hung with shelves of clay teapots and iron trivets, a floor of scuffed wooden planks. Dust floated through rays of sunlight, glittering. Aside from the register—which was plastered with stickers promoting anarchy and burlesque and emcees and marijuana—the countertop was furnished only with ikebana and bonsai in stone pots. The arrangement of flowers, the cultivation of trees, both could be forms of art, just like hacking. Sensei said that there were no superior or inferior forms, that every form had something to teach us about our own. Before sensei had taken me here, I had never even known the teahouse existed.

The teaista was leaning on the register, eyes shut, nodding off.

<body> updo furrows <object>mascara</object>
eyelids cheeks lips <object>pencil</object>
<object>lipring</object> throat collarbone
<object>blouse</object> wrists knuckles
fingernails </body>

She had a habit of chewing pencils, which her sister nagged her about constantly. Today she had felt like wearing a sweater, but also had felt gross, had overslept and then had woken "feeling hideous," and consequently "vulnerable," and "pathetic," and "weak," and so had chosen the blouse, with its petite bow and its buttoned cuffs, instead. As "fashion armor," to protect herself "from the world." She had messaged her roommate about borrowing the blouse while biking to the teahouse. Her sister nagged her about that too—typing while biking—along with snorting while laughing, and reading while cooking. She often confused, in her messages, than and then, affect and effect, loose and lose and dessert and desert. She misspelled the names of celebrities. She used emoji and emoticons unsparingly. Her comebacks were inspired.

By the time the door had shut and the chime hanging there had jingled, her features had updated, her eyes fluttered open. She set the pencil on a newspaper—an unfinished crossword, eraser shavings clumped together at the creases—and yawned, then grabbed a menu from the stack. I chose the table in the corner, nearest to the outlet, settling onto a wobbly stool, and, without speaking, only pointing, ordered a lemon currant scone and a cup of matcha. Wearily, she took away the menu.

Sunlight had warmed the tabletop. Even in here you could smell the thawing. While the teaista heated water in the kitchen, I plugged in and powered on my computer. The elderly couple was finishing the remains of a sesame cookie, pinching crumbs from a plate.

Before doing any work, I searched online for signs of sensei.

His sites hadn't been updated. No posting, tweeting, blogging whatsoever. Just the same old post from five weeks before: "who yearns for gyahaha and kyahaha?" The same tweet: "all your brain are belong to us!" On his blog, the same entry, the same title: "on capitalisn't and communisn't." Were these his final words? Were there double, triple, quadruple meanings? Was some message hidden there, in anagram, in cipher?

Probably there was no hidden message, only single meanings, his typical offhand remarks.

One by one, I logged in to his accounts. Acquiring his passwords hadn't required any hacking. Like the keys, sensei had given me his passwords two years ago, back when he had agreed to become my sensei. His passwords were all in leet: "l1b3r7y," "3qu41i7y," "ju571c3." Very sensei. A pain to type.

Nothing had been downloaded from or uploaded to his storage account. He hadn't bought anything, anywhere. Nobody had accessed his email account, except for me, yesterday.

So then sensei was still missing.

I put the screen on screensaver, slumped back against the wall, watched pigeons with speckled plumage hop around the patio beyond the windows. Where had sensei gone? Before vanishing, he had been at work on assembling a botnet of absolutely staggering proportions for a coordinated attack on the stock exchange. We belonged to a collective of anonymous hacktivists. At marches and protests we all wore masks of the same identical goateed face. I had my mask in my backpack, currently, zipped in with notepads and textbooks. Sensei had left his mask in his bedroom, lying on his nightstand, along with his computer. Sometimes I worried I should have been trying harder to find him. He had no relatives, except for those in cemeteries. He had no friends, only associates. If I didn't find him, nobody would. But what else was there? What else could I do?

If he was dead, I would probably never recover.

The dingy velvet curtain that separated the kitchen from the parlor ruffled. The teaista brought out a copper kettle, a stoneware bowl, a linen cloth, a bamboo whisk, an ivory scoop, a tin of matcha, a plate with a scone. Balancing everything, she wore the grim focused expression of an acrobat performing a tightrope maneuver famous for killing acrobats. She relished the danger—the teetering bowl, the slipping cloth—and took pride in her ability to carry numerous objects simultaneously, to serve "any order, no matter how large, in one trip," although she also felt "dumb" about being proud of "something so ordinary." She stepped gingerly across the parlor, skirting tables, nudging chairs.

One by one, she installed everything onto the tabletop, except the kettle. "Here's your tea," she said, in a casual voice, avoiding glancing at me, trying to hide the thrill she didn't know I knew she felt. I did like matcha, but that wasn't why I always ordered matcha here. I always ordered matcha because I knew that making matcha, preparing that specific tea, was what she considered her "reason for living." I loved watching her remember that.

She began. Throughout the procedure her movements were elegant, precise. Tipping the kettle with a flourish, she poured a splash of water into the bowl, spilling nothing. She waited for the stoneware to heat—testing with fingertips, touching the bowl, impatiently—then dumped the water out. With brisk swoops, she dried the bowl with the cloth. Then, swiftly, while the stoneware was still hot, she scooped matcha into the bowl, a quick flick of bright powder. Again she tipped the kettle, pouring water over the matcha, almost filling the bowl. Then, finally, she whisked the mixture, fiercely, in a zigzag motion, until the matcha frothed.

Afterward—still gripping the whisk, squinting into the sunlight—she took a moment to scrutinize her handiwork, standing gazing at the bowl. To her my presence there meant nothing. Whether anybody drank the matcha was meaningless. Whether I, in tasting the matcha, managed or failed to recognize her achievement, her degree of mastery, was meaningless. What had meaning was the act itself. She had prepared the tea perfectly.

"So, there you go," she said, without looking at me. She massaged her neck—with stiff arched fingers, at the spot where her skin met her hair, lately she had been suffering from pains there—then carried the kettle, the cloth, the whisk, the scoop, the tin, back through the curtain, scowling proudly.

I sipped the matcha, nibbled at the scone. The rich grassy flavor of the matcha relaxed my entire body, from scalp to soles, instantaneously. The scone was still warm from the oven—beneath the currant and the lemon, I could taste dollops of butter, streaks of cream, bursts of vanilla, chunks of salt. Suddenly I was very glad to be alive in this nation, with this teahouse, in this body, with this tongue. Well, enough about ecstasy. I got to work.

I had homework—an essay for econ, a poli-sci exam to study for, something due soon for history—but, like always, I shelved the homework in favor of hacking. I didn't care if I flunked out of college, if that was what becoming a hacker took. I would have sacrificed anything. Weekdays, I trained seven hours per day. On weekends, I trained closer to eleven. With sensei gone, my progress had slowed—for every breakthrough, there were countless setbacks—but that only made me more determined to keep training.

The past few weeks, I had been working on a script, a program designed to hack the servers of a private hospital in Connecticut. I was stuck though. The script didn't work. I couldn't figure out what was wrong. I had spent days already poring through the lines of code, looking for the problem. The script seemed functional. The script was broken. I had never attempted to hack anything on the scale of a hospital before, and the potential consequences terrified me. A hospital would have honeypots, honeytokens, deadly network security. The script didn't just need to work. The script needed to be perfect.

I was troubleshooting—posting queries, skimming tutorials—when the chime jingled as somebody stepped through the door.

The teaista peeked from the kitchen into the parlor, smirked; her sister had come to visit, carrying a paper sack.

This was an incredible bonus: I hardly ever got the chance to see her sister in person.

They chatted at the curtain—about the weather, an obscure musician, an upcoming wedding. Her sister told an anecdote about lactating, which made the teaista laugh, then snort. Her sister pretended to be horrified. "If you want to get asked out, that snorting has got to stop!" her sister clucked, shifting the paper sack. The elderly couple—perhaps prompted by the anecdote about lactating—was gathering a pair of jackets from the hooks along the door.

The teaista headed toward the counter with her sister. They made plans to visit the cemetery tomorrow for the anniversary. Beforehand they would buy a bouquet for the grave. Her sister had to go, waved goodbye, swung open the door, and walked out—then walked back inside. "I almost forgot!" her sister cried, rummaging through the paper sack. Manga emerged—the cover tattered, pages warped with water damage—a new volume, which her sister had bought that morning, briefly used as a coaster, dropped once in a gutter, obliterated a spider with, and already finished reading. "You won't believe what happens!" her sister hissed, waving the manga. The teaista snatched it, then shooed her sister toward the door, clutching the manga as if afraid her sister might try to take it back.

Her sister left again, hollering goodbye. The elderly couple paid, carefully buttoned their jackets, and hobbled out. After that we were alone.

She read manga at the register, flipping pages with a steady

rhythm, occasionally smiling or pouting. I typed code on my computer between bites of scone. The rays of sunlight rotated across the teahouse as the sun crossed the sky. She didn't know me, anything about me, couldn't have cared less about my presence there. But, for me, there was something very powerful about the experience. Some days this was my "reason for living." Just spending time together, quietly, in the same room.
</html>

<html>
Later that afternoon a gale blew in a skyful of dark indigo clouds tinged with gray. A toddler in a colorful parka creaked past the teahouse on a tricycle, in reverse, not even touching the pedals, getting buffeted straight backward by the wind. By then the teaista's shift had ended, and I had missed all my classes. Yes, grades this semester were going to be dismal. I ordered some takeaway, kukicha, which was prepared by the teaista's replacement, a tattooed man with a blinking tic. Sipping the tea, huddling into the warmth of the paper cup, I hiked from the teahouse to the nearest metro station. The subway car was crammed with total strangers. I sat there, swaying when the car swayed, jerking when the car jerked, lurching when the car lurched, watching everybody. People in trenchcoats, beige, charcoal, navy. Slumped women sighing murky patches of steam into the scratched windowpanes. Kids in caps, gripping binoculars. An elderly woman hugging a painted canvas wrapped in plastic. I could view the bodies, but didn't know what was in any of the heads. It broke my heart. I wanted access.

My whole childhood, bouncing from foster home to foster home, my dream had been to become a hacker. You could learn the basics online, but advanced techniques required a teacher, a master of the craft. Sensei was legendary. He had hacked military installations in Louisiana, agricultural companies in Nebraska, banking conglomerates in Virginia and Minnesota and Pennsylvania, had written enchanting bewitching scripts that could snare the heart of any computer, revolutionary masterpieces of code. Every skiddie had heard of him. So when from my sophomore dormitory, through a combination of basic hacking techniques, I had blundered onto what seemed to be sensei's billing address (for a plush bathrobe from an online merchant) and had realized that he lived, not only in my state, not only in my city, but only a few neighborhoods beyond campus, I grabbed my lanyard with its keys and tumbled out the doorway and ran without sneakers wearing only socks through a dawn fog down streets coated with pale gold and dark gold and bright scarlet leaves, and, panting, sweating, trembling, rang the buzzer for his apartment. A typed label taped under the buzzer revealed the name of the tenant hidden within. Sensei's name was unusual enough I was almost certain the tenant was him. And I had heard recordings of sensei's voice, manifestos on hacktivism that every skiddie had memorized, delivered by a gruff fiery voice with foreign undertones, and when that voice spoke to me from the speaker above the buzzer, then, then, then, I was absolutely certain. The voice told me to get lost. I begged the speaker to accept me as an apprentice, and after that the voice went silent. I rang the buzzer, again and again and again, and was given no response. Then, a returning dogwalker let herself and her pug into the building, and I slipped through the door and snooped around the stairwell and found sensei's apartment. I knocked. Through the flimsy wood of the door, sensei shouted at me to go away. For seventeen hours I knelt on the straw mat there, head bowed to the mat, palms spread across the coarse straw fibers, in the dark, listening to raindrops thrumming against windows, the pattering of footsteps as other tenants came and went, the pipes thocking within the papery walls of the stairwell, trying not to nod off, silently begging to be accepted, until, around midnight, sensei tripped over me as he left the apartment with a bulging bag of trash. "What, you, still?" sensei cried, splayed backward across the landing, covered in potato peels and lemon rind. The bag had split. He gave me a broom to sweep the trash, which had been my first chore.

Sensei's motives were political. "Our government's been hacked by corporations! We have a duty to hack them back!" Despite his age, and his health, he considered himself a vigilante, "not unlike a caped crusader." He had once sworn to me that he was "going to save the planet, and this nation, and at least a billion children." I really admired that, obviously. My motives were completely different though. For me, hacking was social. I just wanted to find people to love. Sensei considered this ambition "idiotic." Stepping from the subway car to the underground platform, I was struck by a vision of sensei pacing his kitchen with that mask of the goateed face hanging from his neck as he scolded me, "You're wasting your time! You've got the talent to make something happen!" Remembering that lecture made me miss him.

Aboveground, flags were snapping against flagpoles. People whose faces were wrapped with scarves hustled across the crosswalks, hunched forward into the wind. Downtown was busy, even for downtown. I could smell the sea: saltwater, and that rich loamy smell that gathered in the depths of empty seashells, abandoned homes. The wind cut through the worn khaki of my coat, making me shiver. I tugged the hood, lined with fur, over my head.

In the porthole windows of a candlelit pub, a retired electrician I followed was splitting a foamy pint with the man he loved who didn't yet love him. In the lavish offices of a glass skyscraper, an overworked editor I followed was firing a subordinate whom she thought of as a son, which she had been dreading nauseously for days. In the dim backseat of a braked sedan, an unemployed scion I followed was revising jokes for a stand-up routine he performed every weekend at a local club, under a stage name. They weren't who I was looking for. I kept trekking. Past dappled horses towing carriages of beaming tourists, past vendors sprinkling fried dough with powdered sugar, through windswept alleyways and vacant parking lots.

Until there she was. A girl on a deserted playground, perched in the shadowed hollow of a concrete tube. The blader. What was in her head just then? The same thing as almost always.

<head> daydream </head>

Whenever she daydreamed, she would take on a certain expression, part squint, part glower, completely glazed over. That was the expression she now wore. She had been sick, so couldn't breathe through her nose, was breathing through her mouth instead. She lay sprawled against the side of the tube, staring out and up at the sky, with the shadow draped across her body like a blanket. She was highly active digitally—wrote notes to herself on her phone, used scores of social apps, frequented chat rooms and message boards under pseudonymous usernames. I had discovered the subject of her daydreams while hacking her. Her daydreams followed a single theme. Trying to imagine what her parents might look like, sorting through the infinite possible versions of those faces—infinite, but all variations on her own face, that face now being displayed to me.

<body> bangs irises <u>cheekbones</u>
snubnose <i>teeth</i> <s>chin</s> neck </body>

Then a mob of boys on skateboards clattered into the playground and chased her from the tube, shouting twisted versions of her name.

She hurried off, not rollerblading, instead clutching a skate in each hand. Earlier today she had ripped her jeans and scraped her knees. The scar, that pink lump struck across her chin, was from a fall too, though years before. Her sweatshirt was the same size as mine, for a body half the size, and she wore no coat. Her adoptive parents had offered to get her braces for her teeth any number of times, yet she "totally refused," for reasons that she herself didn't fully understand but that were likely related to her daydreams: protective of her face, not wanting to change a thing, if that was her only clue to the faces of her birth parents. She tripped on a crumpled magazine, kicked at a pecking seagull, hurried across an intersection of honking trucks. I followed at a distance, sipping kukicha. The city was made of mirrors: shimmering windows, domed bells on the handlebars of chained bicycles, bent bumpers on parked taxis, polished brass address plates on marble columns, curved mirrors above banking machines, swinging glass doorways, ticketed glass windshields, glass smudged with handprints over posters billing upcoming movies, cracked glass over expired advertisements. I watched without watching, my reflections following her reflections. She wasn't as easy to love as the teaista. The blader was very, very, very angry. She insulted everybody, constantly, including herself, and hated everybody, consistently, including herself, and used both racial and gendered slurs. Once she had noticed me reading a textbook in the park, had not particularly discreetly snapped a photo of my face with her phone, and later had posted the photo to her blog with a caption mocking my birthmark. But, also, I understood why she was angry. When I was her age, I had been very, very, very angry too. Her daydreams were "a new thing." She had "just never really thought" much before about her birth parents. Now she wanted, "needed," their identities. Her adoptive parents didn't want her to know though, had told her that once she was an adult she could do anything she wanted, but that until then their decision "was final." I saw what they didn't. Not knowing was killing her. She wouldn't last until she was an adult—by then the anger would have eaten her alive. In her life she had overcome only ordinary obstacles: bullies, influenza, spurned crushes, an appendectomy for appendicitis, the trauma of witnessing a deer suddenly get slaughtered by a minivan on the highway. She was unexceptionally heroic, which seemed exceptionally heroic. To watch her skate was heart-stopping.

She crossed an overlook at the edge of the park, trotted down a steep zigzag of stone steps to the plaza below, and settled onto a bench. This plaza was her absolute favorite spot for skating, and the overlook my absolute favorite spot for watching. But tonight, rather than lacing into her skates, she slumped backward, facing away from me, off toward the common. Lost herself in daydreams again. Brooding. I sat on the overlook high above, resting on a stone railing blemished with blackened splotches of spit gum. The blader was the reason why I hadn't given up yet on the script—the script I had been troubleshooting at the teahouse—the script I was writing to hack that hospital. The script was maddeningly, humiliatingly, brutally difficult. I would have quit trying to figure it out weeks ago if it hadn't been for her. But I couldn't let myself quit. She had been born in that hospital. I was trying to get her the names of her parents.

She still hadn't moved. She was especially moody tonight, even for her. I wished I had something that I could drop for her to find—a vintage track ribbon, an antique war pendant, anything that she might like—but I had only my backpack, with my mask and my computer and my notepads and my textbooks, and my now empty paper cup. I didn't have any cash. I didn't even have a coin.

I glanced toward the stone steps, where a vast flock of pigeons had gathered, silently, as if amassing forces on the eve of some coup.

I tightened the straps of my backpack and rushed at the flock with a growl, sending the pigeons hopping, then waddling, and then with a frantic loosing of beating wings leaping into flight.

It wasn't much, but was enough.

Below, the blader rose from the bench—watching as shapeshifting flickering networks of pigeons shot across the plaza, a lopsided smile forming on her face, awestruck—and then stuffed her feet into her skates to join all that whirling movement.

I left the blader there. I was ready now to head back toward campus. I was starving. I threw my cup away, hiking off into the park, toward the nearest metro station, which was across the common.

The wind had died. The seemingly imminent rainstorm had dissipated, leaving a frigid twilight of scattered clouds. Glassy puddles of snowmelt glinted on the path. The oaks and the elms, leafless, were transforming to silhouettes. Stars were revealing themselves. A satellite.

After what had happened with the pigeons, I was feeling very content, was feeling really calm, and so was completely unprepared for what happened next.

Crossing the bridge over the lagoon, I realized that somebody was chasing me.

Somebody in a black suit. Clacking along the pavement. Clutching a swinging briefcase. Wearing a mask of a pale, flushed, goateed face.

I stopped, stunned. I realized, then, that some part of me had never expected for me to find sensei—that some part of me had always been waiting for sensei to find me.

Why was he running?

Would we have to run somewhere together?

I gripped the railing, bracing myself for whatever was coming next.

He reached the bridge, shoved between a pair of women with strollers, bumped a jogger, stumbled, glanced back, kept running—there was a moment at the center of the bridge when his tie touched my sweatshirt, our bodies were linked—and ran on past me, bolting toward the park gates.

My entire body had gone weak. I felt crushed: initially, as he flew past, because I believed that sensei had failed to recognize me; then, watching him running away, because I realized he had never been sensei at all. Even if the hair was a toupee—sensei was completely bald—the length of the ears, the width of the shoulders, the height of the legs, were all wrong. The posture. The gait.

And, obviously, sensei had left his mask behind.

</html>

<html>

I rode the subway back to school, ate a bowl of stew in the cafeteria, printed a history handout in the library. Before leaving, I got online to check the people I followed. The air outside was damp and tart and crisp. Somebody had draped a kimono over the statue in the courtyard. Kids toting liquor bottles, dribbling basketballs, giggling into phones, were streaming into the dormitories. I rented a studio, off campus, alone.

Leaving campus, I spotted a pair of goateed masks—that same face—hanging from the bushes, as if dumped there by fleeing hackers. Or maybe tipsy partiers, ditching costumes, stumbling off to some hookup. If the hacktivist collective had held an event tonight, I hadn't heard.

Dusk had come. My breath had turned to clouds. I was exhausted. As I walked, my head was bent at the sidewalk, viewing nothing but cracks and stones. Mentally, I scrolled through the things I'd learned at the library. The teaista was eating salted popcorn ("organic!"), watching what had been her mother's favorite movie, preparing for the anniversary. The blader was getting a skate with loose wheels repaired by her parents ("they've got no clue what they're doing but they're trying anyway"). The mail carrier I followed had survived knee surgery. The bank teller I followed had survived heart surgery. The rooftop beekeepers I followed had found a shop that might sell their honey. Everybody was still here. Boston had survived another day.

Shuffling past the building where sensei lived, I heard a mewing. The tabby cat darted from the alley between the pawnshop and the pharmacy, across the street, over the curb. Before I could even speak, it brushed against me, rubbing my shins through my jeans, mewing again.

This attention wasn't unwelcome, but was unusual, definitely. Aside from mealtimes, the chef usually just got ignored. And typically petting of any sort was strictly verboten. Tonight, though, something seemed different. I decided to try. I knelt. The tabby came around, nudged straight into my hands.

As my fingers ran along its back, its spine arched, following my fingertips. The tabby was trembling, as if scared almost.

I glanced at the building where sensei lived—noticed, on the fourth story, the window was glowing. I stopped petting the tabby. I stared at the window. I knew that light—that certain pinkish luster cast onto the kitchen ceiling through the patterned lampshade on the lamp. Either I had left the lamp lit, or somebody had broken into sensei's apartment.

The tabby bolted.

The warped monstrous shadow of a body slid across the kitchen ceiling.

Somebody was breaking into sensei's apartment.

I ran, yanked the hood of my coat over my head, didn't need the keys that sensei had given me—the door was ajar, a squirrel had crept into the building to inspect the rug in the entryway, I leapt the squirrel and launched myself up the staircase hitting only every other step and with the railing used my momentum to whip around the landing on the second story sending a mat there skidding and launched myself up the staircase with my backpack thudding against my back and with the railing used my momentum to whip around the landing on the third story almost overshooting nearly throwing myself into the overgrown ferns some tenant kept potted there and slipped and cursed and recovered and launched myself up the staircase, but then froze—panting, crouching, suddenly thinking, I took the last few steps to the landing on the fourth story very quietly, so I could ambush whoever had broken into the apartment rather than getting ambushed myself.

The door to sensei's apartment was ajar too, record albums scattered across the futon, rumpled sweaters strewn across the floor, a mirror overturned, the drawers yanked from the

cupboard and lying upended haphazardly in the hallway—
sensei was getting ransacked.

Then—the exact moment I heard the voice, muttering, a
gruff fiery voice with foreign undertones—I saw him, in the
kitchen, hunched over a duffel bag.

Sensei was getting ransacked by sensei.

"Sensei?" I said, shoving down the hood of my coat.

He yelped, fumbled something, whirled about.

What was in his head just then? Exactly one thing I wanted.

<head> answers </head>

"Where have you been?" I said, stepping into the apartment
over a pair of clayey boots with frayed laces. I felt intensely relieved that he was back—but, also, weirdly upset that he had
made such a mess of the apartment. For five weeks this place
had been spotless.

"You're here, you're here, you're here!" sensei murmured,
rising up, throwing the duffel bag over his back. He clapped
my elbows with his hands. I had forgotten how tiny his body
was.

<body> scalp wrinkles brow <object>bandage</object>
<object>eyeglasses</object> nose
<s>dimples</s> stubble mouth shoulders breastbone
nipples <u>ribs</u> navel hips
<object>belt</object> <object>slacks</object>
ankles veins toenails </body>

A broom tipped, clattered to the floor, and he gasped and
flinched and leapt back from the noise. I hadn't seen him like

this before—he was usually very calm, never edgy. He tossed the duffel bag onto the counter and began rooting through a drawer. He had a limp, I noticed. A teacup containing a last swig of tea sat by the lamp on the table. Genmaicha, from the look. Very sensei. As frantic as he seemed, he had taken the time to make a pot of tea.

He stuffed a rusted can opener into the duffel bag.

"Kid," he said.

"What happened to your head?" I said.

"It's the end of the world," he said.

"Why are you limping?" I said.

"The meteors are falling, the tsunamis are coming, the volcanoes are about to blow."

"You haven't even been blogging," I said.

Sensei hurried into the hallway. "The blog," he laughed, bitterly, muffled, his head stuck in the depths of the closet. "The blog's finished."

"What do you mean, finished?" I said.

"I'm shutting it down," he called, pulling a brown wool cap onto his head, rushing into the bathroom. "I'm shutting it all down."

In the bathroom, he reached into the cabinet and stripped an envelope from the underside of the sink. That cabinet beneath the sink was where I kept all my cleaning supplies. Somehow, though, I had never spotted the envelope taped there.

"Did something happen?" I said.

He was back in the kitchen, had crammed the envelope into the duffel bag.

"I want you to know that I'm proud of you," he said. He yanked his arms through the sleeves of a cardigan, shook the cardigan on. His mask, his computer, his jacket lay jumbled together in the duffel bag. A metal flashlight. A toothbrush with kinked bristles. I noticed suddenly what he was doing. He wasn't unpacking. He was packing.

He zipped the duffel bag.

"You're leaving again?" I said.

"Listen, where I'm going, you can't follow," he said.

"I'm coming with you," I said.

"I need you to promise me you won't even try," he said.

I hurled my backpack at the futon.

"I'm supposed to be your student!" I shouted.

Sensei buttoned the cardigan. He tugged on a pair of fingerless gloves. He hesitated. Then he finally looked at me.

"Your training's over," he said. "You're a hacker now."

I couldn't speak. I should have been happy. Instead, I felt like I'd had some terminal diagnosis and had just been pronounced dead. I didn't want to be a hacker, if that meant that now sensei could abandon me.

Sensei selected a chipped porcelain teacup with an indigo design from the shelf of teacups above the table. The tabletop was marked with overlapping pale halos, burned into the wood by the countless cups of tea that had been set there without saucers, as many mine as his. He placed the teacup at the nexus of a few halos. With his back to me, he tipped the teapot, pouring steaming genmaicha from the curved spout into the teacup below, until only drips were left, and then not even drips. The surface of the genmaicha shimmered in the glow of the lamp.

"That's the last of it," he murmured. "This cup's yours."

He patted my elbows, stomped into the boots in the doorway, threw the duffel bag over his back, and then was gone.

The thoughts and feelings in my head then, they would have broken most machines. I collapsed into a rickety chair, slumped backward, tried and failed to raise my head. I felt like yelling, but couldn't. I felt like crying, but couldn't. The lamp had given my coat, my jeans, my sneakers that certain pinkish luster. The tiles were littered with dropped spoons and fallen socks. The radiator was creaking. Outside, a siren wailed, swelled, faded.

There was some voice in my head. This is the very last tea sensei ever made for you, it said. So this here is the most important cup of tea in the history of the world. You'll have to pay extra careful attention as you drink it, and remember everything about it. And savor every sip. Okay? Hey, hacker? Are you listening?

I wasn't listening. For a very, very, very long time I stared at the floor. As it happened, I ruined my farewell gift—by the time I came to again, my tea had gone cold.

</html>

The Golden Mean

A.

Tryg spent the week, like every week, in the suburbs, lounging in the hammock with his mother, bouncing on the trampoline with his stepfather, choreographing plays with his sisters, sneaking cookies from the cupboard with his sisters, building a hopscotch course with his sisters that had numbers chalked into the squares and spanned the length of the driveway and included multiple routes and by design took the shape of a fractal, doing homework, and reading, and, that whole week, his empty duffel bag lay in a crumple by his bedroom door, never letting him forget that eventually he'd have to leave. The duffel bag was made of a camouflage material, with his name embroidered beneath the zipper in cursive, and had a canvas strap. The mere sight of that bag would send a jolt of despair spiking through him. He couldn't enter or exit his bedroom without passing it. It haunted him. He waited for the microwave to heat his oatmeal, leaning back against the dishwasher, trying not to smile as his mother read puns aloud from a magazine, and afterward, when he brought the bowl of oatmeal into his bedroom, there lay the duffel bag. He rooted through gelato in the freezer, searching for a certain flavor, cracking up while his stepfather did impersonations of coworkers, and afterward, when he carried the bowl of gelato into his bedroom, there lay the duffel bag. He burrowed into the throw pillows on the window seat in the living room, wearing thick woolen socks, watching the ceiling fan whip about in blurry ovals, listening to mingled voices as his mother recited credit card pins into the telephone in the hallway and his stepfather called out sports scores to a neighbor from the porch and his sisters debated whether what rainbows were was actually just friendly lightning, feeling cozy and warm and very content. And later, in his bedroom, there lay the duffel bag, reminding him that he couldn't stay, that his days there were numbered.

Then, the weekend came, that quickly the weekend came, and as the sun began sinking through the clouds outside his bedroom window, he stood over the duffel bag, feeling a sense of doom.

He packed it. Just threw things in, helplessly, resigned to his fate. In went his textbooks. In went his graphing paper. In went his compass, his protractor, his calculator, his ruler. Clothing wasn't necessary. Neither were toiletries. He already had all that where he was going.

Tryg was in-between age-wise—not quite child, not yet teenager—a pudgy, clumsy, nervous creature who routinely slaughtered standardized tests. He was taking calculus at a high school. He counted everything, instinctively, avoided doing anything in uneven numbers, obsessively, and, from memory, could recite the first hundred decimals of π. His only serious crush was on ∞. His sense of fashion was logical to a fault, favoring comfort over style, loose crewnecks and baggy slacks, shoe inserts for arch support. He read mathematics journals for recreation.

He had two families: the Appelbaums and the Bergquists. Privately, he referred to them as Family A and Family B. Family A had members {Mom, Stepdad, Tryg, Natalie, Isabel}.

Family B had members {Dad, Stepmom, Tryg, Elliott, Parker}. They were separate families, but together they were his family, A ∪ B, {Mom, Stepdad, Dad, Stepmom, Tryg, Natalie, Isabel, Elliott, Parker}. He was the only member of both sets, the only intersection, A ∩ B, {Tryg}. That was what defined him. He had the largest family out of anyone and was the most alone.

Family A lived out in suburbia.

Family B lived on a farm.

His mother was shouting for him to hurry.

Tryg dragged the duffel bag out of his bedroom, down the staircase, and into the brightly lit expanse of the living room, full of despair. The sunset tinted everything. Back during the flood, so much rain had fallen in the suburb that even with all the windows latched shut the water pouring from the gutters of the house had seemed to roar. Tonight the windows were all propped open, letting the breeze in through the screens. The weather was unseasonably mild for autumn in the Dakotas.

Dinner was cooking in the kitchen, emitting a savory smell: roasting meat, root vegetables, crusted with herbs and dripping with oil. Candles were lit at the center of the walnut table in the dining room. The places were already set. His spot was bare. No napkin, no cup, no fork, no knife. Just a blank stretch of tabletop. Seeing that, he felt a spasm of misery. He didn't want to eat at the farm. In the living room, games were stacked on the tufted ottoman—card games, board games, dice games—and the printout coupon that had been stuck to the refrigerator was gone, replaced by a pair of movie rentals tucked discreetly into the painted cabinet that housed the television. Anguish swept through him. At the farm, there would be no games, there would be no movies. Tomorrow his mother and his stepfather were attending a banquet at the museum, some heritage event with ceremonial awards and plattered appetizers. His sisters would be dancing in costume. He'd miss that too.

Tryg dropped the strap of the duffel bag and then collapsed onto the carpeting, leaning back against the leather sofa, burying his head in his arms. He could feel the rolls of his gut folding over in a series of creases, with the bottom curve pressing against the buckle on his belt. He peeked over his wrists.

"Can't you just say that I'm sick?" Tryg muttered.

"You would still have to go," his mother said.

His mother was rooting through a purse in the hallway. Her dress was striped, her nails were painted, and her hair was damp from a shower. Her shoes were already on, the ragged tennies with the splitting seams and the permanently discolored soles that she only wore when she knew she wouldn't have to get out of the car. She worked as an engineer, was an unapologetic germophobe, and had been a lifelong advocate of wind energy, birds be damned. She snored at night, a comforting drone that drifted through the house. The sound helped him sleep. Nights at the farm were eerily quiet in comparison.

His mother wrested a ring of keys from the purse with a jingle, threw open the door to the garage, and then turned back toward him, holding the door open at 45°.

"We've got to leave."

"Not yet," Tryg said.

"We're already late."

"Just wait," Tryg begged.

In the kitchen, his stepfather, who was still wearing a suit from the firm where he worked as a paralegal, had slipped on polka-dotted oven mitts to check the temperature of the prime rib in the oven. His stepfather had his glasses tugged down from the bridge of his nose to the tip, the way he always did when the glasses were giving him a headache. Something extraordinary was, his stepfather could juggle. Also, his stepfather was multilingual. His stepfather always made very confident, deliberate, smooth movements. Even watching his stepfather do something as mundane as remove a thermometer from a drawer could be pleasant somehow. Being around motions like that made him feel totally secure. No one at the farm moved that way.

His stepfather pivoted away from the oven, ± the thermometer, he couldn't tell.

"Tryg, buddy, do you want us to save you some leftovers?" his stepfather called.

"It won't be the same," Tryg mumbled.

His sisters (half-sisters technically), shy red-haired girls whose faces and limbs were spotted with freckles, were perched on the window seat. The breeze coming through the bay window rustled their clothing, checkered blouses and khaki shorts. Natalie's body < Isabel's body, yet, oddly, Natalie's head > Isabel's head. They had been passing the time until dinner looking at activity books with hidden objects in the illustrations. They set the activity books aside, drawing their knees up to their chins, wearing concerned expressions.

Generally his sisters were too proper to ask personal questions, but, overcome by curiosity, his sisters dared to ask some now.

"What will you do there?" Natalie said, tentatively.

"Be bored out of my mind."

"Is there a hammock?" Natalie said.

"There's nothing."

"Is there a trampoline?" Natalie said.

"There's nothing."

"You don't like anything there?" Natalie said.

"The house is depressing, the food is terrible, and there's nothing to do."

"What about your other family?" Natalie said.

"I hate them and they hate me."

His sisters considered that, glancing at each other, and then turned back to him, looking worried.

"What if the hopscotch washes off while you're gone?" Isabel said.

Tryg stared at his sisters over his wrists, unable to answer, upset[loyalty]. He knew his sisters were bothered by the thought of him belonging to another family. His mother and his stepfather were the same way, tried to hide how they felt, but they didn't like having to share him either. They didn't like him missing things. Among the matrix of family photos above the fireplace hung pictures he wasn't in, taken at events he'd been absent from, as if he'd been just blanked out from certain moments in the family history. There were episodes from the family lore that he knew only as stories, family jokes that referenced incidents he hadn't shared. It didn't matter whether an experience the family had was positive or negative. Ultimately the |experience| was enormous. If any pictures were taken at that banquet at the museum tomorrow, he'd be missing from those too. He dropped his face back into his arms.

"I don't want to go," Tryg shouted, emphasizing it for some reason, he wasn't sure why.

His sisters didn't get math. Even at their age, they at least should have understood the basics, addition and subtraction, multiplication and division, but they were hopeless. They flunked their assignments. They bombed their quizzes. Numbers made no sense to them. He loved that about them. He loved that his sisters would peer at him timidly from his bedroom doorway, too mannerly to enter until they had been invited, when they came to him for help with worksheets. He loved that his stepfather had a sneeze so powerful that if he was standing out in the driveway sipping an iced lemonade while his stepfather was sorting through dusty boxes down in the basement, and all the doors were shut, and all the windows were shut, he could still hear the sneeze from out there. He loved that his mother sang oldies while she was sweeping the kitchen sometimes, unprompted by anything, would just suddenly break out into song, poking him in the ribs to annoy him. He loved when the family was crammed into the bathroom together, his stepfather drying the hair of this sister, his mother snipping the nails of that sister, him squeezed between the sink and the toilet just trying to brush his teeth. He loved the suburb, everything about that house, the walls painted in bright citrus shades, the gleam of the marble counters, the decorative goblets filled with shells and corals, the tiled motif of triangles and quadrilaterals that surrounded the bathtub. He flopped backward across the floor, digging his fingers into the carpeting, trying to savor everything he could about the place while he still had the chance. He was stalling, there was no way of getting out of going, but every additional second he managed to delay seemed priceless. He hated that the other family was allowed to take him away from here.

Once, flipping through the newspaper, searching for the funnies, Tryg had stumbled onto an article about a local man who for years had lived a double life, secretly, with two separate families. Tryg had reeled. Who would ever voluntarily choose such a thing?

He had been a newborn, zero years old, at the time of the divorce.

This had been his situation his whole life.

His mother pointed into the garage, swinging the door open to 90°.

"We really need to go," his mother said.

Tryg got into the hatchback, lashed himself with a seatbelt, and wrapped both arms around the uneven lumps of his duffel bag, peering over the top. He watched in the mirror as the garage door separated into individual slats divided by fissures of sunlight, which, following the tracks, gradually combined back into a single door on the ceiling above the hatchback. The radio murmured pop music. Leaving the suburb, his mother, whose current state = preoccupied and whose driving record ≠ amazing, nearly plowed over a cat with a collar that was crossing the street. His families lived on opposite ends of town. If the city was graphed, using miles for coordinates, with the axes expanding from an origin downtown, his mother lived at $(-1.2, +3.1)$, his father lived at $(+1.3, -3.4)$. That is, north-north-west, south-southeast. Per the visitation arrangement, he spent [Monday, Friday] with his mother and [Friday, Monday] with his father. Every week. He had suddenly remembered so many things he wanted to talk to his mother about, things to ask her, things to tell her, he'd had days, he didn't know why he'd wasted so much time just sitting around listening[polite], because there were things he urgently needed to say. Clutching the duffel bag, he turned to her, opening his mouth to speak. But saying anything seemed impossible now. The pressure—having a deadline, a countdown ticking away to a moment when he'd be cut off from his mother entirely—panicked him. He'd never say everything in time. He turned away from her, closing his mouth again, distressed. Businesses whipped past: strip malls, grocery stores, gas stations. An inflatable bison advertised the price of snowmobiles. Someone in a uniform swept the walkway of the motel where back during the flood the evacuees had gotten to stay for free. His mother seemed to have forgotten the speed limit, maybe had forgotten there even were such things. He felt a sort of desperation settle onto him as the hatchback carried him increasingly farther away from where he wanted to be. Why should he be taken from people he loved to go stay with people he hated?

The exchange always occurred downtown, in the parking lot of a convenience store. Neutral territory. As if he were a prisoner of war. Which, in a sense, he was. The pickup had beaten the hatchback there. Skaters with fauxhawks lounged against the dumpster, sipping from to-go cups, squinting at the vehicles, as if present to act as witnesses. Someone had dropped a slushie, which had melted into a puddle of neon on the asphalt. The dumpster was so full of garbage bags that the lids couldn't shut.

"See ya soon," his mother said, leaning over to kiss his forehead.

Tryg hesitated, then removed his seatbelt, distraught that this final moment with his mother was slipping away.

Lately, in his leisure reading, he had been studying ratios. Ratios were about relationships. Relationships between numbers. There was a certain ratio, known as the golden mean, that especially captivated him. The golden mean often appeared in nature: the branches of trees, the curves of shells, the scales of pineapples, the seeds of sunflowers, the spirals of genomes, the dimensions of bones, the bodies of galaxies, the trajectory of falcons, the ancestry of bees. It had been used in the design of drawings and photographs and paintings and sculptures. It was considered the most beautiful proportion in the universe. Expressed numerically, its first nine digits were 1.61803398.

Reaching for the handle of the door, he suddenly thought to calculate something. When he did, the result was staggering. Between weekdays with his mother, weekends with his father, alternating holidays, and periodic vacations, the time he spent with his families roughly approximated the golden mean. On average, 4.3 days per week with Family A, 2.7 days per week with Family B.

If that was true, shouldn't the situation have seemed beautiful, instead of so ugly?

B.

On the outskirts of town the parking lots and utility poles gave way to fields and trees. In the pickup, he said nothing, just stared out through the streaked sheen of the window, furiously, watching what passed: the farm with the weather vane; the farm with the storage tank; the farm with the basketball hoop with the rusted net. At the camp of prefabs where the oil workers lived, someone was pounding on a door, wearing coveralls spattered with black gold. Earlier that week a tornado had swept through, and the crumpled wreckage of several trailers lay at the edge of the camp, hadn't yet been hauled away. Farther down the highway, roadkill bloodied the side of the road, the remains of some raccoon or skunk. Twilight was falling. Dust billowed as the pickup swung into the gravel driveway. When he climbed out, his father was still talking, rambling^boring.

"Welp, we certainly missed you here this week," his father said in conclusion, slapping the pickup, then reached to take the duffel bag.

IIis father wasn't a farmer, actually worked as an electrician, but was the type of person who was always consumed with some new hobby or another, and over the course of his childhood had transformed the property into something that ≈ farm. A sunroom extended from the back of the house, where misters on automated timers watered containers of vegetables, carrots and squash and radishes. A hut stood near the garage, a coop for the chickens, who were nowhere in sight. Beehives in painted boxes sat on cement blocks down by the woods. Unexpectedly, as the smell of compost hit him, he was struck by a wave of euphoria. He squinted. The feeling confused him.

"You're here!" Elliott grinned, grabbing him by the cuff of a sleeve, her mouth crusted with bits of dried jam, and then suddenly she was running, dragging him by his crewneck, leading him down past the ferns through the woods to the creek. Parker was there, throwing rocks at a squirrel while she waited. His sisters (half-sisters technically) were pale blond-haired girls with spindly frames who chattered so excitedly they often interrupted their own stories. Elliott was wilder, generally bandaged from some scrape or cut. Parker was sneakier, but always got caught. In the fading light, the trees were gray, the mushroom caps appeared bright white. His sisters splashed barefoot across the creek, yanking the legs of their jeans up to their knees, shoving the arms of their tees up to their shoulders, as shadows × and ÷ over their bodies.

"Let's do this thing!" Parker cried, throwing her hands up, flashing victory signs.

Tryg frowned. He'd forgotten. The weekend prior, he and his sisters had lugged buckets of paint down from the garage, an assortment of colors, and painted a target onto a boulder by the creek. Concentric rings rippled out from the bullseye at the center. Numbers marked the annuli between circles, indicating the value of striking the target there. Near the boulder lay salvage he and his sisters had taken from the garbage can: wine corks, rusted nails, melted spatulas, empty lighters. Each type of object had also been given a certain value, which, together with the value of the spot where the target was struck, determined the points scored for a throw. Tossing stuff at the boulder had actually been fun addicting.

"You won't believe how good we've gotten," Elliott said.

"We're talking bullseyes every time," Parker said.

"We made up some new rules," Elliott said.

"You're going to love the one about bottle caps," Parker said.

As his sisters squatted to choose projectiles, his father, standing somewhere up near the rain barrels by the slider door, shouted that dinner was ready.

"But we're doing the target thing with Tryg," Elliott yelled.

"You got all weekend," his father shouted.

"Tryg doesn't want to wait though," Elliott yelled.

"It's too dark for that now anyway," his father shouted.

His sisters bolted toward the house, chanting something about food.

Tryg trudged back through the woods, baffled by what had happened at the creek. Slipping into the house through the slider door, he discovered his duffel bag perched like a trophy on the laminate counter in the kitchen. His stepmother, who worked as a paramedic, and recently had turned vegetarian, had a gingham apron on over jeans and a turtleneck.

"Tryg, honey, do you want pop or milk?" his stepmother asked, squeezing his shoulders as she swept past toward the dining room.

His sisters had already claimed seats at the rectangular oak table, and were now poking the palms of their hands with the tips of their knives, testing the sharpness. His father switched on the same disc of swing music that always played during dinner, snapping his fingers. His stepmother hung her apron from her chair. A ceramic container sat on a crocheted potholder at the center of the table. He sat down across from his sisters, eyeing the thing suspiciously. His stepmother lifted the lid, revealing macaroni and cheese topped with a layer of crushed crackers. It smelled astonishingly delicious. His stepmother generally served the meal once ⟨visit⟩. Something about the smell of the meal and the sound of the music and the sight of these faces was affecting him oddly. Euphoria swelled in him again, a kind of ecstasy. That and a sense of foreboding.

As he chewed, he snuck glances at the house, examining everything, stunned revelation. He'd missed this stuff. He'd missed the dishes, the colorful swirls on the rims. He'd missed the utensils, the clear plastic handles shaped to look like beveled glass or cut crystal. He'd missed the placemats, which were quilted, with a stitched pattern of astroids and deltoids. He'd missed everything about the place, the wildlife calendar in the kitchen and the landscape watercolors in the hallway and the musty smell of the carpeting and the curtains that matched nothing except each other. He loved the way his father squinted with satisfaction when bending down to sniff a fresh scoop of food, wrinkles forming around his eyes; he loved the way his stepmother would grind the pepper mill high above the table, letting the seasonings tumble dramatically down onto her plate, as if daring someone to intercept some flakes; he loved the way his sisters would swing their legs under the table while they were talking and kick him accidentally and apologize and stop talking and sit very still and then moments later start back up talking and forget to sit still and swing their legs under the table and kick him again and when they realized what they'd done burst out laughing and sometimes laugh so hard they forgot to breathe. He was a traitor. He was a two-timing, double-crossing, no-good fucking traitor. He didn't hate coming here. He didn't hate this family at all.

How could he have forgotten? Did this always happen? Was the way he'd thought he felt just a lie he told himself so he could tell the lie to his other family?

"What did you do this week?" Elliott said through a mouthful of noodles.

"Just boring stuff," Tryg said.

In the article in the newspaper, there had been a blurry photo of the man who led the double life, taken perhaps from online. A trucker with plain hair and an ordinary face. Beneath the photo, the man was quoted, "I just, I dunno, always felt really lucky, having twice as many people to love."

Tryg tossed the duffel bag into his bedroom after dinner, put away the folded laundry on his dresser, threw on a polyester jacket from his closet. He was ecstatic. He could barely contain how happy he was being back again. The coyotes were howling. The temperature had plunged. The moon was 62% shadow and 38% light. His father dragged the firepit out of the garage and built a blaze in the backyard, marching around proudly with his hands wedged into the pockets of his jeans, squatting occasionally to blow a gust of breath into the logs to fuel the flames. His stepmother leaned back in her fold-out with a plaid fleece blanket wrapped around her legs, pointing at the stars, inventing constellations, giving each a mythology. He set marshmallows on fire with his sisters. They removed the charred exteriors with their fingers, plucked the stuff into their mouths, chewed the ashy sugar, and bit off the gooey interiors whole. Then lunged around the campfire, shouting mock insults, fencing with their branches. He was ecstatic—but that wasn't all, because as his sisters chattered back and forth, he caught references to things the family had done over the course of the week, without him, earlier that week his father and his stepmother had taken his sisters to the hardware store to pick out a new birdfeeder together, and he hadn't been there, earlier that week his father and his stepmother had watched from the edge of a track as his sisters had strapped on fluorescent helmets and ridden dirt bikes for the first time ever, and he hadn't been there, earlier that week his father and his stepmother and his sisters had huddled in the basement with flashlights and can-teens and weathered the tornado in a state of utter terror, and he hadn't been there, he'd missed everything, he couldn't be anywhere without creating an absence elsewhere, he was even less a part of this family than the other one. He was on the run now, fleeing jabbing branches, heading toward the road, laughing, but beneath the laughter, beneath all the delight and the joy and the pleasure, there was something else, something that was always there, a sadnesssadness. He was only a fraction of a son. He was only a fraction of a brother. He would never be whole to them like they were whole to each other. He would never be whole to anyone.

Movements

I. Allegro
(or, Fanatically Obsessed with Trivial Arguments)

I became trapped on the roof around midnight, wearing only an undershirt, heart-patterned boxers, cloth slippers, and a terry bathrobe embroidered with the logo of the hotel. I was exhausted, had wanted only to sleep, but after stripping off my button-down and chinos—staring at that empty bed—a feeling of oppression had taken hold of me, the wallpaper seemed unbearable, the carpeting seemed intolerable, the air in the room suddenly seemed both too thick and too thin, yes, both, simultaneously, which may be difficult to imagine, but the point is that the air was stifling—I felt as if, without fresh air, I would suffocate, I would die. At my age, sudden bodily emergencies like that had become remarkably common. Knotting the sash of my bathrobe, I fled the room, hurrying down the hallway, where discarded platters smeared with streaks of pesto and ketchup lay waiting for housekeeping, and the wallpaper and carpeting were just as distressing. Thumbing, repeatedly, the button to summon the elevator from the lobby—already dreading having to pass the shrill wails of the apparently never-ending singer-songwriter gig underway in the hotel lounge in order to reach the revolving door that separated the lobby from the street—I happened to glance farther along the hall-way, and noticed a doorway that led to the stairwell, labeled, "Roof." Aha! What luck! I'd avoid the singer-songwriters after all! I slipped into the stairwell and climbed quickly, steady-ing myself at intervals with the railing. The door at the top of the steps was admittedly plastered with what may have been a warning, but in the land of lawsuits, where warning signs seemed to have become as rife as billboards, who ever both-ered to read such things? I stepped out onto the rooftop, the door shutting behind me with a hollow thunk {*forte*}. I found myself in a moonlit landscape of spinning vents and steaming pipes. The sky, flecked here and there with stars, had a violet glow. Brisk summer air rushed over me, sweeping away every trace of oppression, leaving me with a sense of calm. I breathed, deeply, fully, gratefully. For those wishing to picture me, imag-ine a lofty, rather svelte man, dignified by wrinkles, eyes ac-cented by horn-rimmed glasses with mottled frames. My jaw-line was chiseled. My cheekbones were prominent. My hair, luxuriant, textured, a bright glossy silver, remained streaked with darker strands. I was, frankly, a handsome creature. But hark! Within this charming body lay a wretched soul. I soon recovered, breathing that rooftop air. I would sleep. I would sleep. I felt wonderful—I strolled back to the door with a skip in my step—I felt suddenly quite wonderful—until twisting the knob and discovering that this side of the door was locked. Discovering that, I didn't feel wonderful at all. I was shocked; I twisted the knob again, giving the door a shake, forcefully; yes, truly, this side of the door was locked. Whose fool policy was this? Was it a security measure? To keep out intruders? What sort of far-fetched break-ins was the hotel expecting? Burglars scaling the building wearing face masks and suction cups? Thieves strapped to parachutes pitching out the cargo bay of an airplane? The hotel stood twelve stories, a chromatic scale of modern architecture! None of the adjacent buildings stood anywhere near as high! A cursory search revealed the rooftop had no other doors. That door was the only door, and the door was shut fast. I cursed {*fortissimo*}. I cursed {*sforzando*} again. I redid the sash of my bathrobe, which at some point had come undone. At the edge of the roof, I sprawled across the tar, peeking over the ledge, heart beating at a dizzying tempo—I'd always been a coward about heights—and was reminded that none of the rooms had balconies. There was nothing to drop down to, aside from the pavement twelve stories below. I was trapped. Beneath the hotel, tourists and townies strolled the sidewalk in colorful apparel, traversing the grooves between slabs as if crossing the bars between measures. At the stoplight, a taxi was honking {*mezzo-piano*} at a pickup that was honking {*mezzo-piano*} at a trio of apparently wasted pedestrians who had abruptly halted halfway across the crosswalk, blocking traffic. Across the street, bass thumped {*piano*} monotonously from honky-tonk bars with neon signage. A one-man band hunched under the crisscrossing straps of an accordion, a banjo, a harmonica, a bugle, a tambourine, a whistle, a pair of cymbals, a range of drums, and an outrageously patriotic display of flags was perched on a crate, yelling {*pianissimo*} something through a megaphone. The winds muffled everything. I lay there trying to decide whether tossing a slipper would be a sensible way to signal my distress to the people below, or if from this altitude a falling slipper might strike some passerby dead.

Beau, my husband, had died the week earlier, felled by a stroke at our kitchen counter; at breakfast, he'd nudged aside his plate of omelet and spinach, lowered himself meekly to the countertop, whimpered {*piano*} once, sleepily, shut his eyes, and never woke again. Beau had been a shy, kind, somewhat chubby man, whose idea of paradise had been a wool sweater, a warm spot of sunshine, and a battered paperback; he'd liked his books so aged the pages were as brittle as the peel on a bulb of garlic and as fragrant as the cloves. He'd been trained as a sculptor, but never found success, and been content working odd jobs, collecting tolls and bagging groceries. When we'd met, he'd had a head of lush, dark, wavy hair, although soon his hair had begun to thin, and he'd been bald ever after, topped by a shiny dome with slight ridges and faint dimples. We had lived together nearly half a century, which had given us ample time to become fanatically obsessed with trivial arguments; among our various disputes, we'd had an ongoing quarrel about traveling. Beau, homebody that he was, nevertheless had a streak of adventurer, and delighted in experiencing new places. At the time we met, we had both spent exactly one year overseas. Beau had spent his year backpacking with college friends, roving without plan from country to country—Portugal, Spain, France, Belgium, Germany, Denmark, Morocco, Algeria, Nepal, India, Bhutan, China—rarely staying in any given city for longer than a smattering of nights. As for me, I had spent my year studying in Vienna, and had never left Austria. That illustrated the difference between us perfectly. Our motives were identical: Beau had been prompted to embark on the backpacking excursion by a desire to "get to know somewhere new"; I had chosen to study abroad because I had fallen in love with Vienna, from afar, through its music, and had wanted to get closer to it, to understand it intimately. Neither of us had been sightseers; we'd had no interest in snapping photos of landmarks and monuments; we'd craved an experience with meaning, depth, authenticity. On that we agreed wholeheartedly. Where we clashed was in our methods.

I didn't believe anybody could come to "know" a place after a mere night bunked down in some hostel. I had spent a year in Vienna; I had devoted my weekends to exploring its districts, had availed myself of every parade, every ball, every festival, had frequented the museum courtyards and palace gardens, had immersed myself in the operas and ballets; I had seen the city in its autumn finery, its winter cloak, its spring frippery, its summer rags, had seen it through both windstorms and rainstorms, had seen its darkened alleys lit suddenly by fireworks, had seen its streetlights suddenly extinguished by blackouts; even then, I felt that I'd barely even begun to understand the place. On the spectrum from "unknown" to "known," to me the city had still seemed very foreign. Beau, however, didn't believe in such spectrums. "It's not either you know it or you don't know it," he'd once argued {*legato*}, propped up naked in bed, his face awash with moonlight, his body in shadows, as steam rose from his mug of chai. "Everybody knows it. Just, differently. That's what makes traveling so meaningful. There are things about a place an outsider sees that a local just can't." He'd had a timid, reedy, lilting voice, and always smiled while arguing, patient but insistent; I'd had a temper, and interrupted him constantly, drowning him out with my brassy timbre. Throughout our relationship, Beau had periodically taken spontaneous trips to random places around the country— his last had been to Smyrna, in Delaware—and in conversation often referenced his experiences in these locations. To me, weekend getaways like that seemed futile, a waste of time. If forced to travel, visiting somewhere for the debut performance of a new symphony—Atlanta, Chicago, Houston, Cleveland—I never bothered to venture out into the city, just shuttled to and fro between hotel room and concert hall. Beau had never given up trying to sway me. The weekend before he'd died—

that was when he'd taken that trip to Smyrna. I remembered him lumbering out of our apartment, carrying his usual floral-patterned duffel bag, with a tomato sandwich packed for the bus. As always, he'd invited me to come. I'd stayed home to compose.

I'd spent decades tormenting him with counterpoints, assailing him with arguments, disputing his every opinion out of principle; now that he was gone, I wanted only to please him. Was that human nature, or a failing specific to me? Regardless, the evening after the funeral, slumped on our bathroom linoleum, drunk on cocoa and marshmallows—at my age sugar was as intoxicating as alcohol—I'd resolved to take a journey: a spontaneous trip to someplace I'd never been. After some deliberation, I'd chosen Nashville, Tennessee. Why there exactly? Nashville was our Vienna: the American "Music City" to the European "City of Music." Beau, I thought, would have liked that touch. I was finally ready to give his theory a chance: to test for myself whether you truly could come to know a place in a single night, the way he'd always claimed was possible. Honestly, I was probably also embarking on the trip in order to postpone having to mourn him—I frantically needed something to distract me—at the time, grieving him seemed an unimaginable task, just impossible.

I arrived in Nashville at dawn, with a ticket to depart the following morning. I dropped off my suitcase at the hotel, ate some waffles and bacon in the hotel lounge, and hailed a taxi. My spirits were soaring—I was determined to give my all to this!—and from there the day was a disaster, although not from lack of trying. I saw about every sight the city offered. I rode a flatboat through the meandering canals in Opryland, jammed onto a bench across from twin toddlers in souvenir ballcaps who competed at kicking me. I rode a carriage through the dusty thoroughfare on Broadway, getting struck in the face by a plastic bag that was blowing about like a tumbleweed. I took a stroll along Music Row, which proved to be just a neighborhood, only a neighborhood, recording studios in converted bungalows, with nothing to do or hear. I examined the Ryman, inspected the Schermerhorn, unexpectedly saw a Parthenon. I didn't stop there; I was searching for some authentic insight into the inner workings of the city; I was prepared to trespass if necessary. I peeked into a yoga studio, observing, with some bewilderment, the inhales {*piano*} and exhales {*forte*} of the contorted yogis, before being thrown out by their pigtailed guru. I scoped out a bridal shop, gawking, with utter horror, at dressmakers sewing {*tremolo*} sequins to a gown in a paisley motif, until getting shooed away by their bejeweled overseer. I paid a cover charge to enter a billiard hall, watched drunken nurses in hospital scrubs nail {*staccato*} darts into a bullseye with sober accuracy, and then had a pint of ale spilled onto, into, my loafers. I intruded upon a laundromat, a pawnbroker, a florist, the waiting room of an accountant. I perused historical plaques, nihilist leaflets, sentimental graffiti. I stumbled upon a concert in a park, listened to off-key cover bands crooning {*falsetto*} the opuses and opuscula of folk and country, cringed through every last ditty and ballad, felt out of place, and tripped over a picnic basket on my way out. By dusk, I'd gotten nowhere. In a last-gasp attempt, I turned my attention to the culinary scene. What sort of fare was eaten here? I tried the sushi. Horrible! I tried the paletas. Terrible! I tried the coffee. What kind of coffee did this city brew? Abominable, that's what kind! Gourmet, with subtle notes of pecan and toffee! A masterpiece of java! Without any warning, I found myself becoming teary, moved by the flavor! I hadn't asked for this! From coffee, I wanted caffeine and caffeine alone! I'd never ordered emotions! Admittedly, the tears were probably somewhat due to my frustration over how poorly the trip had gone. The barista had claimed the cafe was housed in what had once been a pet shop; seated in my booth, thumbing tears from the creases at the corners of my eyes, I listened carefully to the clamor {*fortissimo*} there, hoping to detect, somewhere in the midst of the chattering {*forte*} humans and clattering {*forte*} dishes, the ghostly echoes of woofing dogs and mewling cats. Alas, even with hearing as trained as mine, I heard only the lone chirp {*glissando*} of a ghost parakeet—which ultimately proved to be neither ghost nor parakeet, but rather a living warbler that must have hopped through the swinging door with a customer, and now, trapped indoors, was hiding beneath a vacant table, peeking out at me from behind a trampled napkin. The taxi back to my hotel ran over a screw, a nail, something sharp, and got a flat; I had to walk the last few blocks.

In summary, trapping myself on the roof of the hotel was a fitting conclusion to my trip. Sitting cross-legged on the tar, draped in that ill-fitting bathrobe, staring out over the glittering neon lightscape of downtown, I was struck by a thought that had visited me periodically throughout the day: what the hell was I doing here?

I knew now what I'd known all along: I was always right; Beau was always wrong.

That thought was interrupted by a sudden creak {*mezzo-piano*} as the door to the roof was thrown open. I whirled. A rescuer! Some champion! Come to save me! A youngish hipster, vibrantly tattooed, clad in plaid and denim, and biting a cigarette—who not only shoved the door open, but stepped through, letting the door slam {*mezzo-forte*} back shut.

"Howdy," she grunted {*forte*}.

"Do you have a key to that door?" I said {*forte*}.

"A what?" she said {*forte*}.

"The door can't be opened from this side," I said {*forte*}.

The stranger squinted, frowned, turned, and gave the knob a twist.

"Well, fuck!" she said {*piano*}.

II. Adagio
(or, Secretly in Possession of Chocolate)

She smoked her cigarette, a series of long, deep, measured drags, and then set about trying to attract the attention of somebody in the hotel. She had a stringy build—looked under-fed—hair bundled into a topknot, ears pegged with piercings, a spindly neck, a narrow torso set onto broad hips. Her tattoos ranged from the whimsical to the belligerent. She'd offered, by way of introduction, only the name Mel—perhaps a diminutive for Melody?—Melanie, Melinda, Melisande?—and was, considering our difference in stature, remarkably intimidating. I was given the sense she probably was capable of murder. She spent an incredible amount of time pounding {*mezzo-forte*} on the door—I'd given up on knocking fairly quickly—eventually quit pounding, swore {*piano*} at the door, stalked off, paced around the vents and pipes, kicked at something, muttered {*pianissimo*} to herself, plucked a nearly empty package of tobacco from her shirt pocket as if intending to roll another cigarette, hesitated, scowled, glared at the door, stuffed the tobacco back into her shirt pocket, and, having apparently caught some second wind, marched back over to beat {*forte*} on the door some more—until she finally admitted defeat, shuffling over to me, pouting, and whining {*mezzo-piano*}, "Nobody takes the fucking stairs."

On some prescient impulse, I'd stuffed a handful of miniature chocolate bars into the pockets of my bathrobe before leaving the room. I sat very still, now, to prevent the wrappers from crinkling. I didn't want her to know about the chocolates, in case we ended up trapped here indefinitely. In a skirmish over resources, I'd have the advantage in height and weight; I'd always been somewhat of a wimp about such confrontations, however, whereas, despite her dainty look, she had the aura of a scrappy veteran.

"This is why, usually, I just don't do responsible things," Mel said {*mezzo-forte*}, tossing the package of tobacco onto the rooftop and squatting to roll a cigarette. "I was just going to smoke inside, blow the smoke out a window or something, but my brother said hey, this room's nonsmoking, this hotel's nonsmoking, this whole fucking building is a nonsmoking fucking place, would you show some respect? So fine, I did, I came outside to smoke, I did the responsible thing, and look where it got me! Stuck on a roof. I should have known this would happen. The universe always punishes you for doing responsible things. I actually know some responsible people—they always have ugly babies. Have you ever noticed this? You know any responsible people? Their babies are ugly, right? Yep, it's hard for some people to accept, but we're living in a universe that's opposed to all forms of responsibility. I should have just gone down to the street, but the roof sounded so much closer, and besides, I hate having to stand outside of somewhere to smoke, being huddled there all alone, with everybody inside watching you through the windows, it makes me feel like, like an outcast, like a reject, like in those video rental stores, how the

porn's always kept in a back room with a curtain that never totally covers the doorway, so that people can peek through at
all the pervs—I feel just like that, like some creep in the back
room of a video store, with everybody watching me thinking,
just look at that loser!"

Her speech appeared to have been meant as an overture to
a lengthier conversation, to my dismay. If there was anything
worse than being trapped, it was being trapped with someone chatty. Her voice had a twangy quality, upbeat, mellow.
She bent to lick the paper, sealing the cigarette shut, then bit it,
then lit it, and stood back up. Her phone reportedly had been
dead for days.

"You're a composer? Have you ever conducted? Hey, we're
kind of the same! I'm a deejay. Okay, not a deejay, but a deejay.
I mean, deejaying isn't my job. For money, I work at a record
store. We sell vinyl, cassettes, whatever, everything. If you're
ever in Alabama, you should swing by. You'll need to wear
pants. Hey, maybe we've even got some of your albums! Probably not though. Anyway, that's just my job. It's sad, but these
days there's a difference between your 'job' and your 'purpose.'
All my friends have this. Our jobs have no purpose. I just stand
at a counter—my job is, when somebody wants to buy something, I ring it up, tell them what they owe, and put the money
in the register. Pointless! There are machines that can do that
now! Besides, we get like a customer an hour! Tops! Basically,
I spend my workdays sitting on a stool, staring at the floor in
a daze. I might as well have dementia. My brother, his job's
at this company designing layouts for junk mail. Pointless!
Nobody wants that shit! You might as well address the stuff
straight to the landfill! He himself, my brother, gets pissed off
when he gets junk mail! Can you even imagine how depressing it is to have to spend all day making things whose very

existence pisses you off? Well, that's his job. At night, though, he's got this letterpress printer, and he makes his own greeting cards—they're so cute, so funny, so weird, everybody loves them! That's his purpose, why he's alive. He just can't make a living doing it. My friends, we all get paid to do these pointless things, and get paid next to nothing for doing the stuff that people really love. That's fucked up, huh? Who came up with this system, anyway? I really want to contribute something to the world though. I mean that. I don't want my life to be, just, meaningless. Nobody does, right? Right. Well, that's what deejaying is for me," Mel said {*mezzo-piano*}, nodding, and then tapped ashes from the cigarette.

She turned away, toward the city, gazing in the direction of a bridge, puffing on the cigarette with marked caesuras between inhale and exhale. She had a brooding look: her eyebrows had furrowed; her nostrils had pinched; her lips were pursed around the cigarette. She seemed to have exhausted her reserves of pluck. I considered excusing myself, hoping to retreat to the opposite end of the roof, to set about avoiding her.

Abruptly, her face lit, and she turned back toward me, looking curious.

"Hey maestro, during a performance, have you ever had that moment?" Mel said {*mezzo-forte*}, giving another tap to the cigarette. "You probably think any idiot can deejay, right? Well, you actually need a lot of talent! You've got to know everything! Key, tempo, all that stuff really matters! It's just like being a composer—except instead of arranging notes into a song, you're arranging songs into a, like, much bigger thing. And you're the conductor, too, you've got your instruments, and you're directing everything, adjusting your turntables, cueing your mixer, monitoring your speakers, triggering your sequencer. What makes all this even trickier is that there's an element of improv, because you can actually see the effect the music is having on the crowd, like, beat to beat, and if something's off, sometimes you've gotta ditch your entire lineup, throw something else together on the spot! Beforehand I always get so nervous that I shake so bad I can hardly walk. You have been to a club before, haven't you? It's a lot like a concert hall, except the audience is dancing instead of sitting, and wearing glow sticks instead of tuxes. Oh, and maybe high. Anyway, have you ever had this moment? Do you know it? You've worked so hard, you're trying so hard, to give the audience a certain feeling—and this person over here sorta feels it, but then loses it, and that person over there almost feels it, but then loses it, there's just these clusters of the feeling, coming and going around the room—mostly, really, nobody's feeling it at all—people are feeling something, maybe, but not the thing you came here dying to give them, that exact specific feeling, no, they're stuck feeling totally separate totally different totally random things, on their own, by themselves, alone—but then, everything shifts just barely, and suddenly there's this unimaginably perfect intersection of volume and rhythm and frequency and the feeling just explodes across the room, and everybody has it—suddenly every fucking person in the whole fucking room has it all at once—there's this moment where they're all feeling exactly what you wanted them to, they actually understand that language your music is speaking, they get it, and feel it, everybody, together, they're outside their bodies, they're the same body, they're yours, and what you're feeling, you, is so powerful and so vulnerable at the same time that you can hardly breathe?"

I was about to deny having experienced anything of the sort—and moreover dispute any likeness between the orchestra and deejaying—but then was struck by the realization that I actually knew what she was talking about. I wouldn't have described it that way, exactly, ever, but I had felt it. As it dawned on me, a grin slowly broke out across my face.

"You do know it!" Mel said {*portato*}, looking pleased. "Hmmm, you really must be pretty good. I've still only ever had that moment just once." She frowned. "Ever since then, I've been trying to get back to that place somehow, but just can't seem to."

She flicked what remained of the cigarette onto the rooftop, ground out the embers, and then rested her hands on her hips.

"Alright, maestro. We've gotta get down from here, toss a message down, a note or something. I'll donate some rolling paper to the cause. You have any pens?" Mel said {*mezzo-forte*}.

"Not a one," I said {*mezzo-piano*}.

"Then we're really fucked," Mel said {*mezzo-forte*}.

"I thought about throwing my slippers, but I was worried I might hit someone," I said {*mezzo-piano*}.

She bent forward, squinting at me.

"Worried? This is an emergency! Who cares if we hit someone? In fact, we should aim for them, that'd really get their attention!" Mel said {*crescendo*}.

In one deft movement, she plucked the slippers from my feet by the toes, and without any further ado—such as looking to see who or what might happen to be below at the moment—flung the slippers over the edge.

Together, we peered over the ledge, watching as the slippers tumbled down past the twelve flights of windows, getting struck at points by gusts of wind. Below, a bearded fellow in a cowboy hat and an athletic jersey was navigating the sidewalk in a motorized wheelchair. At the curb, a duo of cabdrivers rested against parked taxis, facing the street, waiting for fares. The slippers landed in the street—which was empty—flopping to either side of the center line.

The bearded fellow hit the brakes, his wheelchair lurching to a halt. He stared at the slippers; he glanced at the hotel; he stared at the slippers; he glanced at the hotel; he stared at the slippers. He activated his wheelchair and continued on toward the stoplight without looking back. The cabdrivers hadn't reacted to the slippers in the slightest.

"Well, fuck, you really do have to hit these people!" Mel said {*forte*}, sounding almost impressed.

"Should we try again?" I said {*forte*}.

She gazed down at her shoes, beaded leather moccasins.

"I need these or my feet will get cold," Mel said {*forte*}, and then glanced at me, as if daring me to challenge her.

"I was actually just thinking the same thing about my slippers," I said {*forte*}.

"Too late now," Mel said {*forte*}.

She plopped down on the rooftop, wrapped her arms around her legs in a sort of hug, and rested her chin on her knees.

"Maybe my brother will come looking for me," Mel murmured {*piano*}. "Probably not though. The truth is, maestro, I'm kind of a fuck-up. He'll probably assume I just took off without telling him. I've been known to do that sort of thing."

Just then my innards gurgled {*glissando*} ravenously.

"Ditto," Mel grunted {*piano*} at my organs.

I'd have to wait until she wasn't looking and eat the chocolates then.

III. Minuet
(or, Dance of the Invisible Thingies)

We'd met, Beau and I, at a housewarming party for a mutual friend, shortly after returning from our respective trips overseas. I'd been a grave, downbeat, mute of a lad, overdressed in a navy blazer and pastel polo. Crossing the threshold from the porch into the house, I'd ducked into a haze of incense and hashish, pressed through the crowd of gabbers {*forte*}, already regretting coming—and there had found Beau. A somewhat chubby stranger, dancing atop a coffee table—not drunk, not even drinking, just dancing for the pleasure of dancing, spinning around solo, as soul howled {*fortissimo*} from the jukebox in the corner. He'd still had his hair then, wavy, dark, lush. He'd been clad all in black: black jacket, black tee, black jeans, black tennies. He'd been spotlit by the sole lightbulb in the ceiling fan that wasn't burned out. I'd almost pushed on through the crowd. I loathed, had always loathed, polite chitchat, idle chatter; I never engaged with cashiers and servers; I avoided conversations with classmates and neighbors; I never, ever, spoke to strangers. What point lay in exchanging pleasantries with somebody you would never see again? But something about him had intrigued me. I'd felt an urge to know everything about him. I'd yanked his sleeve, demanded his name, critiqued his dancing, criticized his outfit, cornered him against the jukebox, and then begun asking questions, endless questions, a barrage of questions about where he was from and how he voted and what he dreamed about and why he always frowned before sneezing, trying to get a sense of who, exactly, this person was. I'd never lost that urge. The questions hadn't stopped until his heart had.

By now the lit windows of the adjacent buildings had nearly all winked out. Even the honky-tonks had closed. Aside from the occasional warble {*piano*} of distant car alarms, the streets were hushed. Mel had given me her lighter, with the task of trying to signal our distress to anybody who might happen to glance up our way. I sat at the edge of the roof, waving the lighter back and forth through the air, in a steady rhythm, like

some dreadlocked hippie at a music festival. Mel rolled cigarettes until her tobacco was gone, tucked the cigarettes into
her shirt pocket, and then, with the last of the rolling papers,
turned to folding miniature airplanes. The wind had died, letting odors gather again. At moments, I caught whiffs of my
sweat, a bitter vinegary tang. Mel smelled faintly of liquor, with
notes of detergent and gasoline, a surprisingly pleasant chord.
From the roof, which perhaps had been recently recoated,
arose a scent of paint. Even without wind, the temperature was
chilly now. Below, somebody dressed in a bright vest, tramping along the sidewalk hunched under a backpack, possibly
homeless, paused, glanced in both directions—the street was
deserted—crept into the street, grabbed the slippers, and then
hurried off into an alley.

"Do you want to know something funny about me, maestro?" Mel said {*mezzo-forte*}. "I always feel the exact opposite of what you're supposed to. Seriously. The exact opposite
feeling. Like once, back in like kindergarten or something,
I begged my dad for months to get me a puppy. Begged and
begged and begged, nonstop, like, would not shut up. My voice
back then was so high-pitched, it'd cut straight through solid
walls. My dad would be locked in his bedroom getting dressed
for work, and I'd be standing at the door, shouting through,
like, facts about puppies. People with puppies have lower cho-
lesterol! Stuff like that. Totally made up. Anyway, one day, I get
home from school, and my dad's sitting on our steps holding
the cutest puppy on the planet. There wasn't any special oc-
casion. It was just, he'd been setting aside some money from
each paycheck, and finally saved enough to buy it. The exact
kind I'd been begging for—breed, color, the brindle marks
and everything. And I stopped, and I looked at the puppy,
and I burst into tears. Tears! I wasn't, like, overjoyed, or just

overwhelmed, or something. I was actually upset. I didn't want to hold it. I couldn't even look at it. My dad couldn't figure out what was wrong. Can you imagine, being stuck having a kid like me, who bursts into tears when you get her exactly what she's always wanted? Well, it was confusing for me, too! Another time, I was in this singing competition, I was really into choir, I practiced for this thing day and night. I was older, like a teenager then. I wish you could have seen me on this stage. I was pretty ugly as a kid. I had no sense of style. Not having a mom or sister, I missed out on a lot of the basics, which didn't help either. You wouldn't believe how lopsided my braids were. As far as eyebrows, or unibrows, are concerned, let's just say nobody had ever taught me how to use a pair of tweezers. Anyway, my dream was to become a musician, and this competition really meant a lot to me, and pretty much the entire town was there. Well, I got last place. Dead last. I should have been crushed. Instead, though, I felt really inspired. Like the crowd had given me a standing ovation or something. I remember thinking, I want to be a musician the rest of my life. In the pictures of everyone onstage, I look even happier than the girl who won, who by the way ended up eloping with this middle-aged realtor and now lives in a cabin in the desert with their like eleven children. My dad went out of his way to be extra nice to me the next week, cooked all my favorite suppers, brought me to the movies, hardly had me do any chores, but he didn't have to, because my feelings hadn't been hurt at all. Really the only thing I didn't feel totally good about was how backward my feelings were. I've never gotten used to it. Of course, it doesn't happen to me with everything. Minor stuff, like parking tickets or sunny weather, I feel how anyone would. If my flight's delayed, I'm pissed! If a kitten yawns, I squeal! I'm normal about the minor stuff. But the major stuff—well, for major stuff, I always feel the exact opposite of what people are supposed to. And that makes me feel like a freak. I wonder, am I even human, if I feel like this? I think about that kind of a lot, actually. Funny, huh?"

She bent over the rolling paper, biting her tongue with just the tip sticking out, as if concentrating very intently on the airplane she was folding.

"You want to know why I'm here?" Mel said {*mezzo-forte*}, still bent over the airplane, making a crease. "Maybe you already know this, but this city's got one of the top hospitals in the country. For cancer especially. So, my dad moved here a few years ago, to get these really intense cancer treatments. Alabama's got hospitals, of course, but my dad wanted the best care that money could buy. Nashville was kinda perfect, because he wanted to stay close to us too. The drive's really not that far. And after his cancer went into remission, he decided to keep living here. He'd made all these friends—he's really cute like that—other cancer patients, these old guys, who he'd gotten kinda close to. They, like, go out bowling together, or whatever. Take outings to football games, wearing matching shirts. Me and my brother, we drive up every so often to visit him for the weekend. His place is really tiny, so we always stay at a hotel. Tomorrow we're taking him out for pancakes. Anyway, he actually wasn't supposed to survive, originally. His diagnosis was pretty bleak. Stage four, super advanced, the doctors gave him maybe a month to live, and that's if he was lucky. He was supposed to die. He was going to die. He called me to tell me as soon as he knew. I remember, I'd just gotten home, I'm standing there in the doorway with one shoe on and one shoe off, and he calls me, and he tells me. And when I heard the news, do you know how I felt? Devastated? Afraid? Like inconsolable, or something? No. Not at all. Relieved. I felt relieved. I'd actually been having a pretty terrible day, some-body keyed my car, my schedule at work was all messed up, the pharmacy wouldn't give me my prescription—I was feeling very, very bad about life—and then my dad called to tell me that he was dying, and suddenly I felt, like, euphoric. I've actually never taken ecstasy, drugs like that really scare me, but based on the things my friends have told me, I felt kind of like somebody who'd just dropped pure ecstasy: very, very, very, very, very, very happy. After I hung up, I kept thinking, what the fuck is wrong with me? I had to move, I needed to do something, I wasn't paying attention to anything I was doing, I went to the sink and started washing dishes, I went to the counter and started going through the mail, I went to the cupboard and started organizing all the boxes of cereal, I stopped, I looked around, and I realized, I'd left the sink full with all the dirty dishes still somewhere underwater, I couldn't remember anything about even a single piece of mail, and why was I organizing cereal? I was in shock, I guess. Even after the shock wore off, though, I still had that happy feeling. Like, glad. Why did I feel that? I didn't want to, I love my dad, I've never known anybody as caring, as thoughtful, as him, he's always supported me and tried his best to understand me, he's like the most important person in my life, honestly. I'm closer with him than anybody. And I found out he was going to die, and, emotionally, for some reason my response was to feel glad. Oh, I hated myself for that! It's the worst thing I've ever done, it was just a feeling, it's not like you make a decision to feel something, you can't help how you feel, there's no choice, you just feel it suddenly, but still, how do you forgive yourself for something that terrible? Even after his cancer went into remission, even after he was totally fine, I couldn't stop thinking about that feeling I'd had. I still really can't."

I lowered the lighter; a breeze had blown out the flame.

"Do you think that I'm a bad person?" Mel said {*diminuendo*}.

Her tone had changed—hoarse now, suddenly gruff. Glancing over, I saw she had that curious expression again, that genuine earnest look of wanting an answer to a question, but with a strange glint to her eyes; she blinked, and a pair of tears streaked down her cheeks, as abruptly as if just then rain had begun to fall and simply had struck her before me. She wiped the tears off, making quick swipes at her cheeks with the cuffs of her shirt.

"Sorry," Mel said {*piano*}.

She gestured vaguely, her hands still balled within her cuffs.

"I'm just really tired, and sick of being stuck, and want to go back inside," Mel said {*piano*}.

"I spent nearly half a century torturing the love of my life day in and day out by disputing every opinion he had and constantly attacking his every flaw and refusing to pardon even the most trivial mistakes that he'd made and making demands that were obviously contradictory, like insisting that he not wake me up with his cold feet but then also that he never wear socks in bed, completely irrational demands, torturing him, because he loved me, and thus had to put up with my every whim," I said {*mezzo-forte*}.

She squinted, as if trying to decide what to make of that.

"So you're a bad person too?" Mel said {*piano*}.

"Well, I hadn't planned on going that far," I said {*mezzo-forte*}.

Mel turned toward the city, cupped her hands around her mouth, and screamed {*fortissimo*}, "A couple of terrible people are up on this roof!" A gust of wind slammed the rooftop, whistling {*piano*} through the pipes and vents, scattering the paper airplanes. Mel shuddered, wrapping her arms around her legs again. I shuddered too, clutching the bathrobe against my frame. Mel plucked a pair of cigarettes from her shirt pocket.

"Here," Mel said {*mezzo-forte*}.

"I don't smoke," I said {*mezzo-piano*}.

"It'll help warm you up," Mel said {*mezzo-forte*}.

"There's a relatively high chance that smoking that would send me straight into cardiac arrest," I said {*mezzo-piano*}.

"Maestro, you're going to smoke with me, there just isn't any choice," Mel said {*mezzo-forte*}.

Mel smoked her cigarette with panache, her movements as graceful as those of a prima donna or dancer of ballet. I smoked mine warily, taking quick nervous puffs. I did not fear death, but did at least hope to die with dignity, which in that bathrobe would be impossible. What Mel had said reminded me of an incident at the funeral parlor a few days before. The incident had occurred before the funeral, at the viewing, in a room with tasteful wallpaper and subtle carpeting. The casket had been open then; Beau had lain there atop the velvet padding in his best suit and his floral-patterned tie. In the lighting, a medley of ceiling fixtures and floor lamps, the uneven terrain of his scalp had gleamed. His features had been arranged by the funeral director into an expression of calm, the exact look of contentment he'd often had during naps. Outdoors, raindrops had ticked {*pianissimo*} against the windows, then streaked down. Our marriage had been an intimate affair—with the exception of his travels, we'd been inseparable—we hadn't even liked to make trips to the grocery store without bringing along the other. Checkups at the doctor's, cleanings at the dentist's, we'd even coordinated those, gossiping together about other patients in the waiting room. His friends had been my friends; my friends had been his friends; neither of us had been close to our families, but after nearly half a century together, we'd each encountered the whole gamut of in-law kin. I'd expected to know everybody at the viewing. And I had—every last person—with one exception. Standing there alongside the casket, somehow managing to accept the sympathies and regrets of the mourners without going to pieces, I was approached by a squat burly woman I had never seen before. She was garbed in a frumpy tweed jacket, a frumpy tweed skirt, and brogues in dire need of a shining; she had a bob cut, sensationally bushy eyebrows, and a belly like a drum. Panting {*piano*}, she hobbled toward me—she seemed to be in quite poor health—hunched over a cane capped with an amber ball, like the head on a mallet, which she gripped as if without the cane she might simply keel over. She introduced herself, a retired lawyer with a forgettable name, and then explained who she was. Although she'd since moved here, she'd been born and bred in urban Idaho—I was shocked to learn there was such a thing—and, either despite of or due to her inner-city upbringing, in college had developed a fondness for the wilderness. She had met Beau, she said, at the base of a mountain in Oregon, just across the state line. Beau had been alone; she had too; they had both come to hike a trail to the summit. "I still remember, he had these neon sunglasses! The frames were neon! We met at the trailhead, happened to get to talking, ended up hiking to the overlook together! Well, we sat there awhile, then made our way back down, shook hands, and that was that!" She spoke {*mezzo-piano*} in pealing tones—rising and falling in pitch, syllable to syllable, like struck chimes—in stark contrast to the monotone whispering {*pianissimo*} that permeated the reception. I hadn't wanted to like her; I found myself liking her nonetheless. "You stayed in contact after that?" I said {*mezzo-piano*}, trying to be polite. "Nope!" she said {*mezzo-forte*}, sweat beginning to bead on her face now, apparently just from the strain of having to stand. "Never saw him again! Well, until the obituary! As soon as I saw that picture, I thought, that's my friend from the mountain!" She paused, wiping sweat from her face with an embroidered handkerchief. Just then, I was startled by the sound of Beau speaking {*fortepiano*}; somebody at the reception was playing a recording of him, probably over a phone. I was drawn to the sound, and was about to excuse myself, to go search for the source, when she said something that confused me. "I'll never forget when he told me about the dance of invisible thingies!" she exclaimed {*mezzo-forte*}. I frowned. "Pardon?" I said {*forte*}. She tucked her handkerchief away, took a firm hold on her cane, and then cried {*marcato*}, "The dance! The invisible thingies! What he liked to do when his eyes were shut!" I craned forward, frown deepening; what the hell was this woman talking about? "He must have told you about the dance of the invisible thingies!" she laughed {*forte*}. "Somehow we got onto the subject of sleeping. He was a lover of naps, he said. Told me he aimed for a nap a day. According to him, though, sometimes when he lay down to take a nap he'd get distracted by the invisible thingies. There's probably some medical term for the stuff. You know those flimsy clear things that float around your vision? Dots, squiggles, bars, flags, all kinds of shapes, overlapping? If your eyes are still, they just barely drift around, but if you move your eyes, that really gets them whirling. Everybody's got the things. Usually we just look straight through them, don't even notice they're there. Once you remember they're there, though, it's impossible not to see them. Anyway, Beau really liked that he could make the stuff whirl around just by moving his eyes. As much as he loved naps, sometimes he'd end up skipping his nap altogether, and just lie there with his eyes shut, watching invisible thingies. He said, I remember this distinctly, he said that what he really loved was that by moving your eyes you could prompt them to move, but the exact way they'd respond to your cue was unpredictable—you had some control, but they were independent—their dances would always surprise you. He told me he thought that was really beautiful. And, well, I just loved that, when he said it. I never forgot it. To this day, whenever I remember they're there, I'll shut my eyes and make them dance awhile. I never did that before I met him," she said {*mezzoforte*}, and then smiled, as if simultaneously both proud and embarrassed. "A great man," she concluded {*mezzo-piano*} abruptly; with that, she excused herself, hobbling over to the casket. I stood there, stunned. Beau had never, ever, told me any of this. I'd spent my life with him—I'd devoted nearly half a century to exploring his psyche conversationally—I'd known his every passion, every quirk, every habit, every doubt and conviction, every preference and aversion, the landmark moments and humdrum routines of his childhood, the particulars of his relationships with former acquaintances and distant relatives, the specific duties involved with every job he'd ever worked, his elaborate theories about laundry and taxes and spices and karma, the location and dimensions of every impact crater in his psychological topography, the meaning of the faintest shift in his stance or the slightest twitch in his countenance, the secret places he'd hidden sweets to cheat on diets, where he had and hadn't been ticklish, the subtle variations in his signature, the exact cadence of his footsteps, everything,

everything, everything, everything. How many times had he seemed to be napping when he'd actually been watching dancing shapes? How could he have had something like that without my knowing? How could this woman, this stranger, have discovered it in the course of a brief hike—an experience she'd found so meaningful she'd later come to help bury him?

Only now did I connect the incident with what Beau had said about cities: that there were things about a place an outsider saw that a local just couldn't.

I came out of a trance. Mel had smoked her cigarette down to a nub.

"Have you told anybody else about that deejaying moment?" I said {*mezzo-piano*}.

"Basically anybody who will listen," Mel said {*piano*}.

Leaning forward, she tamped out her cigarette.

"What about the cancer diagnosis thing?" I said {*mezzo-piano*}.

Mel laughed {*piano*}, somewhat bitterly, and then stuck another cigarette between her lips, grunting {*mezzo-forte*}, "No. Never. You can't tell people stuff like that, maestro!"

I stared at her profile, a darkened silhouette—heaped hair, flat brow, sloping nose, sharp chin, features that were suddenly illuminated as, after a number of clicks {*staccato*}, she managed to ignite the lighter for her cigarette—thinking, with some awe, I know something about this stranger that nobody else does.

My cigarette had burned down only partly, halfway, but the glow had died long ago, the flame had gone out. I ground it out anyway—thoroughly pulverizing it, in case there were still some spark, somewhat paranoid about fires—and then turned back toward the city, wondering about Beau.

Where had he gone?
Who, or what, was he with there?

IV. Rondo
(or, Simple, Flat, Almost Childish)

It wasn't dawn that woke us, it was the birds that came just before, a flock of songbirds that had alighted on the rooftop and
now were perched across the vents and pipes, preening feath-
ers, cheeping {*piano*} and trilling {*forte*}, on a layover for some
migration, the temperature had eventually grown so frigid
during the night that we'd been forced to huddle together for
warmth, alternating at intervals who was wrapped around
whom, concluding, ultimately, with my body nestled into hers,
her body draped over mine, a hand tucked under my chin, a
hand clutching at my shirt, she awoke with a phlegmy sniff
{*pianoforte*}, a pudgy bird with jerky movements had been
hopping toward us, curiously, and when we stirred the bird
was startled, shrieked {*glissando*} in alarm and beating {*pianissimo*} both wings soared off into the sky, and the other birds
followed, rising in a fluttering {*fortississimo*} mass and circling
above the hotel in looping arcs before dropping back to the
rooftop and settling onto the vents and pipes again, jabbering
{*sforzando*} now. We sat up. Mel yawned {*fermata*}, rubbed her
eyes with the heels of her hands, and blinked wearily, strands
of hair matted against her cheeks, her bangs plastered sideways
to her forehead. I scratched my face awhile. Clouds streaked
the dawn, the colors were muted, a wash of indigo, with notes
of pink and saffron along the horizon, casting a soft muffled
light across the buildings, the sun still hadn't risen yet, but

the city too was stirring again, motorcycles sputtered {*piano*} through the stoplight, a janitor in coveralls dragged rattling {*pianissimo*} trash cans into an alley, a shopkeeper in cowboy boots heaved a security shutter up with a crash {*piano*}, somewhere a jackhammer was slugging {*mezzo-forte*} pavement, a sheet of metal covering a pothole in the street clapped {*pianissimo*} when run over by a taxi, somebody was periodically flinging objects made of glass, maybe bottles, into an empty dumpster, where the glass would shatter {*staccato*}, a bus blared {*mezzo-piano*} a horn at a swerving commuter cranking at the pedals of a bicycle, a semi reversing at a loading dock down the block had begun beeping {*staccatissimo*}, the siren on an ambulance or cruiser suddenly caterwauled {*mezzo-piano*} and cut out, a quartet of musicians, possibly buskers, lugged, respectively, a jug, a saw, a pair of washboards, and a washtub bass past the hotel, cackling {*smorzando*} over some joke, the birds on the vents and pipes behind us twittered {*forte*}, as we sat there together, at the edge of the roof, chewing blearily, sharing the chocolates.

"It's kinda pretty in the morning," Mel croaked {*piano*}, and then laughed {*forte*}, surprised by her rasp.

Once, with Beau, lying in a shady nook in a park, stuffed with crab cakes and ice cream, I had heard a song playing {*piano*} from some stereo—I'd raised myself from the grass, scanning the buildings beyond the fence, greystones, brownstones, looking for the stereo, but instead the song had gone silent, muted abruptly by a shutting window or a closing door as Beau had yanked me back down to the grass to show me something, some toadstool, some caterpillar—I'd never heard the song again, I'd heard only a snatch to begin with, the tune had been simple, flat, almost childish, but something about the melody had captivated me, haunted me to this day. I'd begun studying music in kindergarten, a uniformed stripling in a private school; I'd devoted my life to studying certain symphonies, analyzing the nuances of the dynamics, scrutinizing every slur and accent, memorizing every note and rest and accidental, trying to comprehend the essence of the composition; and that work had not been wasted. Now, though, so late in life, I realized there also had been songs like the song in the park, there had been others, strains caught through the parted doors of a stopped train, airs caught through the open window of a turning car, brief truncated snatches I'd had some insight into as intimate as any I'd ever had with those symphonies.

From our vantage on the rooftop, overhearing that random section of the city at that exact moment, I'd caught one of those snatches. Now that there was daylight, with my bathrobe for a flag to wave, our rescue seemed only a matter of time. But, me, I was content just to sit there—I could have listened to that noise forever—I didn't give a damn if we ever got back down.

Proof of the Century

Wills was sitting in his chair, the chair he always sat in when he sat, the recliner with the broken handle and the exposed padding and the cracking leather cushion. There was a blizzard outdoors. Rather than falling to the ground, the snowflakes were flying in every direction, floating sideways, rising upward, plunging downward, soaring away from and at the window. Snow had built on the branches of the pines behind the ranch, and darkness was falling, so that the window now reflected the glow of the television in the living room. He realized—then remembered—that he wasn't alone in there. He turned. Framed photographs stood on the cabinets to either side of the television. The television was switched to a live broadcast of a football game, on mute, showing a replay of a line judge fetching a penalty flag from the field. None of the lamps had been lit yet, leaving the glow of the television the only source of light, which faintly tinted everyone. The people crammed onto the sofas around him seemed hardly older than teenagers: somebody whose chubby face was spattered with freckles; somebody wearing a sweater over an oxford whose nose had a lump from a break; somebody with tattooed hands whose mess of hair was dyed bright white; somebody in rumpled fatigues with a snaggletoothed gape. Others were sprawled dramatically across the carpeting, or sitting on the fireplace cradling diapered infants. Everybody was drinking from something. Glasses of beer, tumblers of liquor, goblets of wine. Frosted cans of soda. Scuffed bottles of milk. Ignoring the television, chatting back and forth eagerly, some looking rapt, others looking amused. Holding a symposium in his house.

"It's a famous paradox."

"I still don't get it."

"Okay. Here's the basic idea. Our sun is an ordinary star. Our world is an ordinary planet. There are billions of stars just like ours with billions of planets just like ours that are billions of years older. Statistically, intelligent life should exist elsewhere in the galaxy. Like, all over the place. But there are no signs of it. Nobody has contacted us. We haven't detected anybody. It doesn't make any sense. It's a total mystery. Like, if somebody should be there, where is everybody?"

"Whoa, you almost spilled my drink!"

"Sorry but when I think about aliens I get so excited that I just have to squirm."

"Personally, my theory is, we're at the moment of truth. Everything before this was inevitable. As soon as we started making tools, little stone arrowheads or whatever, our trajectory was set. It didn't matter how long we took to get here. We could take our time figuring things out. Now that we're here, though, time is of the essence. We've invented machines that can circumnavigate our planet in a matter of hours, which leaves us disastrously vulnerable to a pandemic, the wrong microbe could kill us off completely, there's no way to contain a plague in the age of express trains and supersonic airliners. We've developed synthetics that are consuming resources and generating pollution at a rate that's eventually going to cause total ecological collapse. We've built weapons that have the potential to annihilate our entire civilization. But—for as advanced as our technology is—our technology is still too primitive for us to start colonizing other planets. That's the moment of truth: that in-between moment when you have the power to destroy your home but aren't yet capable of leaving it. It's a test. When a species finally has to prove itself. Which, in my opinion, is the solution to your paradox. There probably have been civilizations in other systems. The reason we haven't heard from them is that they aren't out there anymore. Those species flunked. All that's left of them are the dead worlds they left behind."

"So you're saying that we're fucked."

"Um, there are babies in the room!"

"I don't know. But without a doubt, this is the moment. All the pressure's on us. Either we'll fail the test and go extinct, or we'll pass the test and get off-world."

Wills shifted in his chair. He had snuck away after the meal, longing for solitude, but the crowd had followed him to the living room. He was desperate to get away from everyone somehow. Family had overrun his house.

He looked at the doorway to the hallway.

If he found his wife, she would bring him someplace where he could be alone.

Wills scooted toward the edge of the cushion. Getting out of his chair had become a struggle. His hands were gnarled into pincers. His knees were swollen as gourds. His back had grown so hunched that whenever he glanced at himself while passing a mirror he always appeared to be on the verge of tipping forward. He was ashamed how he looked. He'd shrunken drastically. The conversation had triggered a series of memories, which struck him all at once, rather than consecutively: as a child, in an airport terminal, wearing bright red mittens, accompanied by a sitter, standing at a bank of windows as a plane taxied away, watching in awe as his parents departed on a flight overseas, which nobody from his neighborhood had ever done before; during college, in a faded denim jacket, strolling past a quiet railroad yard, startled suddenly by the realization that there were freight-hoppers observing him from the depths of a boxcar, migrants with sacks of belongings; as an adult, at a hardware store, wearing mustard work gloves, loading concrete blocks into the bed of the pickup to build a fallout shelter in the basement, being helped by a cashier while his children fiddled with the radio in the cab; after retiring, in a warm fleece vest, taking an excursion onshore during a cruise, feeling a rush of excitement at encountering a turtle on the beach, only to discover upon closer inspection that the turtle was choking on a plastic bag.

Carefully, he pressed his hands into the recliner, shifting his weight from his butt to his legs, and then stood. As a surface the carpeting was unpredictable, often compressing when weight was applied but occasionally holding firm, which made balancing difficult, and the fibers had a tendency to catch on the soles of shoes. He had a cane, which was within reach, propped against the wall, and which he adamantly refused to use.

The people—he lost track of the names—were still talking about extinction.

"How long do you think we have?"

"Before the time's up?"

"There's no way of knowing. Maybe months. Maybe days. At most probably a century."

Wills interrupted.

"Where's my wife?" he demanded.

His voice startled him, came out sounding raspy. The people

on the sofas turned to stare, some with their drinks paused just beneath their lips. Their faces showed a mix of uncertainty, concern, alarm.

"Gramps, do you want to sit down?" someone asked hesitantly.

They had dodged the question. He was afraid they might try to force him back into his chair. Avoiding looking at the faces, he began the trek from the recliner to the hallway, trying to reason out just where his wife would have gone after the meal.

1. Dishes were clattering together $\wedge$ doors were slamming shut

2. There were loud noises $\rightarrow$ she got a migraine

3. There were loud noises

4. Someone reeked of perfume $\wedge$ someone stunk of diesel

5. There were strong odors $\rightarrow$ she got a migraine

6. There were strong odors

7. For a migraine she would want a pill $\vee$ for a migraine she would want to rest

8. She wanted a pill $\rightarrow$ she'd have gone to the bathroom

9. She wanted to rest $\rightarrow$ she'd have gone to the bedroom

10. There were loud noises $\wedge$ there were strong odors

11. She must have a migraine

12. She'd have gone to the bathroom $\vee$ she'd have gone to the bedroom

$\therefore$ She'd have gone to the bathroom $\vee$ she'd have gone to the bedroom

Wills peered down the hallway. To this side, the wall was lined with doors; to that side, the wall was hung with photos. The floor was an expanse of wooden boards that were covered with a woven rug that always tripped him up. He chose his course with care, avoiding the snags and the lumps. Otherwise the hallway was usually clear of obstacles—his wife kept the house pristine—but today a pacifier lay on the rug, and further along lay a pair of pruning shears, and further still lay tape measure in a tangle. Wills was forced to take a meandering route, maneuvering around the debris.

When he got to the bathroom, he stopped in the doorway. Snow whirled beyond the window above the toilet. The light was switched off. The medicine cabinet above the sink was shut. His wife wasn't there.

Initially the bathroom appeared to be empty, but then he realized there were people crouched in the shadows of the tub: a child with buzzed hair, whose knobby brow was bruised; a child with braided hair, whose blunt jaw was scabbed; and a child in a baggy hoodie, holding a neon lighter and a can of aerosol hairspray, smirking.

"You dare me?" the child in the hoodie was whispering to the others, raising the flame of the lighter to the nozzle of the can.

The children noticed him standing in the doorway. They froze, looking guilty. The child in the hoodie hid the lighter and the hairspray below the rim of the tub. They glanced at each other, then turned back to glare at him, and just as quickly as the guilt had come, the guilt had been replaced by looks of defiance.

"We're not doing nothing," the child in the hoodie protested, an inherently true statement.

Wills stared at the children, blinked, turned away, and kept walking.

Further along the hallway he passed a photo on the wall of him and his wife chatting by a mule on the rim of a canyon, him pointing at a map of the trail, his wife taking a bite from a pear. His hands felt clammy, and he wiped his palms on his khakis as he shuffled on down the hallway, approaching the bedroom.

His wife wasn't in the bedroom either. Nevertheless, the bed was occupied. People sat atop the comforter, facing the doorway, with their legs hanging over the bed and their feet dangling above the carpet. Each was hunched intently over a glowing phone. The screens illuminated their faces, casting their wrinkles into relief. Someone had moved his quilt, which was supposed to stay on his side of the bed, over to the side where his wife slept. Someone had dumped a heap of coats onto his pillow. Someone had set a mug of coffee down in the place on the nightstand where his glasses went. Despite that none of them were looking at each other, they were in the midst of a debate.

"I mean, it's tragic what's happened to film. We're the ones who really cultivated it as an art form. And now we're the ones bringing about its demise as an art form altogether. Because we're also responsible for product placement."

"What does that have to do with whether something is art or not?"

"The moment there's a brand name, a film is just a very expensive commercial."

"It's not just in movies anymore. It's in hip-hop, video games, even graffiti. It's like the market has mutated from a healthy form into some cancerous version that's spreading into every aspect of society."

"I honestly don't even notice it."

"I guess you see the same phenomenon with other economic systems. Like in communism, for instance. Except then it's governments seizing control of the culture. Whereas with capitalism, it's corporations."

"Well yeah, that. But also that in communism the pressure comes in the form of a deterrent—prison—while in capitalism the pressure comes in the form of an incentive—wealth—which seems like a pretty significant distinction. Um, to me."

"I mean, if you want the money, fine, then take the money. There's nothing wrong with that. But don't go around making all these claims about being an artist. Just be honest. Tell people you work in advertising."

Out the window beyond the bed, a gust of wind sent built-up snow spilling from the pine trees in waves of powder, as everyone on the bed continued to swipe at phones.

"Do you know where my wife is?" Wills asked.

Everyone looked up at him all at once. Some appeared startled. Others appeared troubled. Most had lowered their phones to their laps.

"Dad, why don't you come sit down in here with us?" asked someone in a silk scarf.

Again, they had avoided the question.

He turned away, then shuffled on down the hallway, leaving the bedroom behind. He was afraid they might pursue him, but after a pause he heard them return to the conversation about art.

Wills had been born with a contradiction in him. As a child, the contradiction had made him feel like he was being torn apart. He used to lie in bed staring at the ceiling in the morning, just focusing on the sensation the contradiction gave him, wondering which urge he would follow that day. Because that was really what the contradiction was, was conflicting urges: both a powerful craving to be good, and an overwhelming desire to do bad. And he knew that the moment he climbed out of bed he would begin encountering situations that would force him to choose.

He was a hefty dark-haired kid with a wash of freckles, only child to a pair of immigrants who were probably the meekest people in Arizona. Although he hadn't met his wife yet, he had noticed her before out roaming around. There was something peculiar about the slant of her face. It made him feel like she was special somehow. Even with as much younger as she was, he thought of her sometimes while getting ready. Splashing his neck. Brushing his teeth. He and his parents lived in a townhouse with lacquered baseboards and monochromic wallpaper. His parents ran a bakery together. He dreamed of becoming a soldier. The country was at war overseas, storming beaches, capturing islands, in an attempt to liberate occupied nations. Posters with inspirational slogans and patriotic images were all over town: posted in stores, tacked up in restaurants, hanging on the walls in the post office, taped up in the windows of the railroad station. He heard new recruits tramping past the bakery cheer, "We're going to save the world!" When he thought about the future, that was who he wanted to be. Someone who saved the world. When he told his parents he was going to be a soldier, though, they brushed flour from their aprons and then broke the news that he didn't have a chance. He had a defect, a faulty heart, which his parents said would disqualify him from ever enlisting.

He was desperate to be some type of hero—he experienced that craving to be good as a type of ache—and he did do some things that made him feel noble. He once gave up a spot in line for the ice cream truck to help a neighbor search for a missing cat. He noticed a dollar somebody had dropped leaving the feed store, and without even hesitating chased the person down to return it. He ran to call an ambulance for a stranger who had fallen off a ladder while everybody else out on the street just gaped in shock at the pooling blood. But sometimes that desire to do bad got too tempting to resist—he'd feel something almost like ecstasy as the possibilities rushed through him— and he also did some things that made him feel diabolical. He once happened upon neighbors tossing sticks at a kid who had just moved in across the street, and instead of intervening, or even doing nothing, he felt a tingle of satisfaction, and he crouched to pick up a rock from the gutter, and he stood, and he threw. He stole a wristwatch left sitting out on a stoop, hid it in a drawer, and never even wore it, took it just for the thrill of taking it. He leaned over a stroller at a barbecue and whispered curses at an infant while nobody was watching. He lied to strangers in a coupe asking for directions. He crushed garbage cans with wrenches. He beat traffic signs with shovels. Climbing the hemlock tree in the alley behind the bakery, he discovered a nest made from twigs and silk ribbon containing a cluster of speckled eggs, which after briefly hesitating he flipped from the branch, watching as the eggs smashed on the pavement below in a spectacle of shell and fluid, with a delayed horror, and later, sitting in the stands at the baseball field, overhearing someone say that humans were the only animals that killed for sport, he felt so ashamed that he left before the opening pitch, and he stepped on a butterfly out of spite while walking home.

Even then, before having learned the formal rules of the language, he intuited the basic grammar of logic. He thought in terms of its lexicon—ifs and thens, trues or falses—attempting to translate everything he experienced into its syntax. There was nothing that frustrated him like an irrational idea. His parents were both devoutly religious, but even as a child he was an atheist, and he refused to tag along to the services his parents attended. The arbitrary credos the minister prescribed, which the congregation accepted without subjecting the claims to any rational inquiry whatsoever, infuriated him. Meek as ever, his parents never forced him to attend, or to bow during their prayers, or to participate in their devotionals. Mornings of services, he stayed home flipping through comics about superheroes in bed. But though he'd rejected the moral code of the church, he wasn't amoral; on the contrary, he was obsessed with notions of right and wrong. A ruminant by nature, he compulsively evaluated the ethics of his every action. His ethical system was simple: if something you did helped someone, it was good; if something you did hurt someone, it was bad. He applied that universally, which caused him all manner of difficulties. He was genuinely confused why anyone would think suicide was wrong—especially if the suicide was ending some type of suffering—a point he raised in class during a discussion about bridges, which earned him both a paddling and, among his schoolmates, a reputation as eccentric. Forever after that incident, whenever he walked home from school, kids taunted him from stoops, making murderous gestures with imaginary nooses and implied razors. He was similarly baffled by how everyone seemed to feel about prostitution—if there was nothing wrong with a boxer getting punched for money, and there was nothing wrong with a masseuse giving rubdowns for money, then there shouldn't have been anything wrong with a prostitute having sex, which undoubtedly carried less risk of injury than boxing and purportedly offered even greater benefits to society than massages—another classroom outburst that not only got him caned but resulted in his schoolmates permanently shunning him. Especially pious kids avoided even looking at him after that, as if he were a known pimp. He didn't have a single friend. The community was almost unanimously god-fearing. Those last few years of childhood were miserable. He seemed to have outgrown everything: his feet hung over the end of his bed; the trinkets he had collected cluttered the floor of his room; his shoulders grazed the sides of the door to the townhouse coming and going; the restless walks he took after supper kept butting up against the borders of town, leaving him standing on the edge of a pasture, staring out at wilderness, ruminating. He was furious, didn't understand how everyone could accept the random dictates of a suspiciously invisible entity, and simultaneously wished that he could have too. He would have given anything to think like everyone else did. Not to feel like such a freak. To fit in. But he wasn't able to ignore the fallacies in the logic.

Incapable of living with an irrational idea, he set about trying to spread the truth, taking every available opportunity to instigate debates with his parents about the existence of god. He felt like, if only his parents thought what he did, he wouldn't care about anyone else. He was desperate to make his parents understand. Over cereal bowls in the kitchen, pinning laundry to the clothesline in the garden, from the backseat of the sedan, drinking lemonades out on the stoop at dusk, he bombarded his parents with rational thinking. That there was no proof that god existed. That the scriptures that were often cited as evidence that god existed were full of contradictions, inconsistencies, and scientifically inaccurate accounts. That there was something obviously irrational about the fact that, whereas anybody in the modern day who claimed to hear a god speaking to them was declared a lunatic and promptly tossed into an asylum, anybody who claimed to hear a god speaking to them in the olden days was considered to have been indisputably sane. For years he harried his parents, using every argument he could think of, never truly believing that his parents would be swayed. Then the miracle happened. He actually succeeded. That final autumn he lived at home, his parents changed. They quit reading verses before bed. They quit praying at the table. They quit attending worship altogether.

Wills felt a sense of relief initially when his parents quit church. That and a sense of accomplishment at having explained his arguments so clearly that his parents had been forced to accept the reasoning. Gradually, however, he realized those hadn't been the only changes. His parents had begun to treat each other differently. He observed these other changes in silence, feeling a combination of panic and confusion. Whereas his parents had once been unfailingly patient with each other, they were becoming quick-tempered, criticizing each other at every turn. His father, who'd always had a cheerful attitude, had become cynical. His mother, who'd always been so earnestly kind, had become sarcastic. At the bakery, they had taken to bickering in front of customers, slamming the register shut for emphasis. Before, they had been selfless, each focused on whether they were meeting the needs of the other; now, they were selfish, each obsessed with how the other was failing to meet their needs. Things only worsened from there. Without the arbitrary dictates of religion—the foundation of their marriage—their relationship collapsed. They never divorced, but they never seemed truly married again, either. He was horrified by the consequences of what he had done. By trying to spread the truth, he had destroyed his family.

Wills was standing just shy of the doorway to the office now.

He glanced up and down the hallway.

He needed to find his wife. That was all he wanted. But she hadn't been in the bathroom, and she hadn't been in the bedroom. By now she might be anywhere. He glowered at the rug on the floor.

He could just yell for her. If she heard him calling, she would come to him. Shouting would be fast. Shouting would be easy. Maybe that was what he should do.

1. He should search for her ∨ he should holler for her

2. Searching for her would be tiring ∧ hollering for her would seem crude

3. She had been born in a shanty

4. Her parents had used shirtsleeves as napkins

5. Her parents had used tables as footrests

6. She was self-conscious about her upbringing

7. She was extremely particular about manners

8. Being associated with anything crude embarrassed her

9. She was embarrassed → she got angry

10. She had become insecure about their children living in megacities

11. She considered their children sophisticated

12. Their children were around → she was especially sensitive about manners

13. Their children were visiting today

14. He shouldn't do anything that would make her angry

   15. Hollering for her wouldn't make her angry

     16. She would be especially sensitive about manners

     17. Hollering for her would seem crude

     18. Hollering for her would embarrass her

     19. ⊥

   20. Hollering for her would make her angry

   21. He shouldn't holler for her

   ∴ He shouldn't holler for her

The corollary being that he should just search.

He could already see that there were lamps lit in the office.

His parents had been right about his heart. War broke out again the summer after he graduated—the country was intervening in a civil war across the ocean now, bombing the hilly peninsula with a staggering tonnage of incendiaries, leaving behind cities of rubble with enemy combatants spattered across the debris in the form of severed limbs and steaming vitals—finally of an age to do his duty, he tried to enlist, but he failed his physical. The military wouldn't send anybody with a defect like his into combat. Instead he got shipped off to college, where he expected to be just as much of an outcast as ever.

His physical had also discovered that he'd developed a visual impairment—pressing his face into the phoropter, gazing through at the chart on the wall as lenses of increasing power had clicked into place, he'd laughed aloud from the shock of seeing how clear the world could be—and he'd taken glasses with him to college, browline frames with pointed plaques. He was full-grown by then, a stocky kid who often skipped shaves, not so much out of laziness as out of a desire to have stubble to run his fingers over absentmindedly. His freckles weren't as prominent anymore. Chairs creaked under his bulk. Given his interest in ethics, he naturally gravitated toward the philosophy department, which was where he was finally introduced to formal logic. He still remembered the moment. The professor adjusting a bow tie. A universe of eraser dust floating above the chalkboard. Wills leaning back in a chair, biting a fountain pen. As the professor began to explain the system at the chalkboard, drawing signs and symbols, working through sample proofs, Wills was struck by a flash of recognition. The realization that here was the language he had been trying and failing to communicate in all along. And that there were actually people who were fluent. He grinned in disbelief, still biting the pen. The feeling was like gazing through the phoropter all over again, watching forms he'd only ever seen as blurry figures suddenly sharpen into distinct shapes. After that he began tinkering with proofs at every available opportunity: in the bathroom, at the cafeteria, in the waiting area at the med center. He delighted in mastering the ability to speak in a mode of pure reason. He took philosophy courses exclusively from there on out.

He had ended up at a college on the coast of California. This was about the time his wife was dropping out of school to run away from home, although he didn't yet know her. A vast desert lay between his university and his hometown. He rarely got to travel back, getting updates mainly via the letters his parents mailed each month. He often thought of his parents during lectures on ethics. Early on his adviser challenged him to consider the theory that ethics were in fact a matter of, not consequences, but intentions. Wills promptly rejected that. Intentions didn't determine whether the outcome of an action was good or bad, and to him, that was what determined whether an action had been moral, was the outcome. Still, other theories weren't so easy to dismiss. As a child, he'd believed that deciding whether consequences were good or bad was simple: if the person seemed happy afterward, he must have helped them; if the person seemed unhappy afterward, he must have hurt them. And in fact there was a theory that held that happiness was the ultimate moral good; however, another theory proposed the ultimate moral good was knowledge; meanwhile, another theory claimed the ultimate moral good was prosperity. When his adviser explained these different theories of moral goods, Wills immediately thought of what he'd done to his parents. He'd never forgiven himself for it, he'd been brooding about it just earlier that morning, but the matter was complicated by these theories. If consequences were evaluated in terms of happiness, then he'd been wrong to debunk the myths his parents had believed, because of the effect on their marriage; but if consequences were evaluated in terms of knowledge, then he'd been right to explain the truth to his parents, regardless of how their marriage had been affected; yet if consequences were evaluated in terms of welfare, then what he'd done was trivial, because becoming atheists hadn't affected their finances whatsoever, they hadn't lost or profited. Wills didn't know how to feel about the saga anymore—guilty or proud or neutral—because he couldn't reason out which moral good was the ultimate.

Personally, he pursued the whole lot in those days, prosperity and happiness and knowledge. He worked part-time at a drugstore in town, earning what seemed to him then like staggering sums of money, leaving him plenty to spare. He drank as much alcohol as possible, played as much chess as possible, ate as many pastries as possible, had as much sex as possible, smoked as many cigars as possible, heard as much jazz as possible, climbed as many roofs as possible to lie there with other students he barely knew and watch meteors fall. He lugged sacks of books back to his room from the library, metaphysical treatises, epistemological discourses, existential manifestos, staying awake on the bottom bunk, reading by flashlight until he couldn't possibly go on, nodding off with the books heaped around him, sleeping just the few hours before dawn. He had never imagined somebody could have so much good. He loved the atmosphere of the university. He dreamed of becoming a professor so he wouldn't ever have to leave.

Wills never even heard of graduate school until that final semester of college. He was in the office of his adviser, sitting in the rickety wooden chair across from the desk. Ostensibly he was there to have his adviser review the latest draft of the thesis he was writing as the final prerequisite for his degree. The thesis attempted to describe the system of ethics he had developed during his time at the school: rather than endorsing a single good, his system recognized multiple goods, an assortment of desirable outcomes that all needed to be taken into account when determining if an action had been moral. The goods weren't equally prioritized, yet the goods weren't ranked, either; instead, the goods had shifting values of importance, changing based upon the circumstances. This system made trying to decide whether an action would be moral vastly more complicated, but to him seemed far more reliable than systems that declared a single good to be the only consequence that mattered. From what he could tell, nobody had ever proposed a system quite like his before. His adviser had taken to calling it "the theory of the century," although whether his adviser was being sincere or wry, he was never sure. Today, however, his adviser didn't seem interested in talking about the thesis at all. Instead his adviser had gone off on a tangent about graduate school. Wills was stunned to learn that such a thing existed. He asked how he could apply, but his adviser only laughed. "Applications were due months ago," his adviser said, moving a stein that had been pinning a slit envelope to the desk. "I applied for you." His adviser removed a folded letter, smoothed the paper across the desktop, and then spun the sheet to face him, a piece of letterhead signed and dated by somebody at a university across the country. "You're in."

Wills left the office in a state of bliss. He mailed the university a deposit, booked a flight across the country, and spent that summer working in the drugstore to save money, glazing over between customers with fantasies of what life at grad school would be like. His desire to become a professor had only intensified now that the dream was actually tangible. He could visualize the exact trajectory he would take to get there, and what awaited at the destination, the articles he would write, the students he would mentor, the lectures he would give, the parties he would host where colleagues would gather to swap ideas and refute old theories and propose new theories and exchange battered tomes embellished with faded marginalia. There was a park with a fountain between the drugstore where he worked and the boardinghouse where he lived, and after getting off shifts he would sit in the sunlight on the fountain eating a slice of pie wrapped in tinfoil, still lost in a reverie, mentally preliving the best scenes of his future. Around twilight he would finally wander back to the boardinghouse, checking his mailbox before lumbering up the staircase to his room. The last letter his parents ever sent to him at that address arrived the evening before he left town. A brown envelope with a pair of stamps that each displayed the face of a president. As he read the letter, crickets chirped out his screen window, and ice cubes snapped in his glass of whiskey. Letters from his parents were usually just a single sheet, but this letter was long, multiple pages. In short, the bakery was on the verge of bankruptcy. His parents were begging for help.

And that was the other moment he remembered, was sitting there on the suitcase he'd packed for the flight to grad school, holding the letter from home. And the despair when he realized what he was going to do.

Wills had reached the doorway to the office.

Arms hanging limp, he peered in.

His wife wasn't in the office either.

All the lamps were lit: the brass lamp perched on the desk, the silver lamp perched on the shelf, the telescope lamp with the linen shade standing between the potted plants. Framed photographs acted as paperweights on the desk and bookends on the shelf. A picture of him and his wife by a pool at a neighborhood potluck, his wife grinning at the camera, dragging a leaf skimmer through the water; a picture of him and his wife in the bleachers at a basketball game, his wife with a lap full of spilled popcorn, pouting at the photographer. Somebody had knocked over the miniature flag he kept on the desk. His pencil sharpener had been shifted. Fluorescent folders had fallen onto the floor.

And there were people, teenagers by all appearances, scattered across the office, engaged in a discussion. A pair lay facing opposite directions on top of the desk, their hands balancing drinks on their navels—a cup of something that looked like apple cider, a cup of something that looked like grape juice—with their knees in their jeans pointed at the ceiling, and their feet in their shoes planted on the desktop. Somebody wearing a loose mesh jersey was spinning in the desk chair, giving the desk a slap every cycle for another boost. Somebody in a furry hat with dangling flaps stood next to the telescope lamp, fingers knotting to form different shapes, casting shadows of animals onto the walls.

"Our pronouns are such horseshit."

"Don't even get me started."

"Our pronouns are total bullshit."

"I seriously can't even believe that gendered options are still like all we have."

"The most primitive fucking linguistic technology."

"I don't want another app update. I don't want another browser update. That shit can wait. Somebody update our fucking pronouns."

"Uh, what's a pronoun again?"

"It's like, people would be so pissed if we had pronouns that distinguished people by race. Like if there were different pronouns for black people and white people or whatever. So that every time you ever mentioned somebody without using their name, you'd have to reference the color of their skin."

"Putting them back in their place, socially."

"It's like, yes, that person has a vagina, yes, that person has a penis, we're aware."

"Like, thanks for the reminder, o holy patriarchy."

"The one with the dick, the one with the pussy, the one with the dick, the one with the pussy."

"Hey, what's a pronoun?"

"And also is like this built-in system to deny the existence of anybody who's genderqueer."

"You're a he, you're a she, or you're a demonically possessed they."

"I'm boycotting pronouns from now on. I just decided. I'm finished with pronouns for good."

"Yo, what's a pronoun?"

"It's something that's totally in favor of people, places, and things."

"Oh. Right. I forgot."

Wills interrupted.

"Have any of you seen my wife?" he asked.

The person in the hat with the flaps glanced at him, freezing in the midst of galloping a shadow across the walls. The person in the jersey gradually revolved to a stop in the chair, staring at him. On the desk, the pair balancing the drinks whispered something to each other, conferring.

"Gramps, do you need help with something?" somebody asked finally.

Wills didn't know why he had even tried.

His breathing had gotten heavy. He was sweating through his flannel. He gazed down at the end of the hallway and the rest of the house beyond.

Maybe he should just wait for her to come to him.

1. She was in the kitchen ⊕ she was in the dining room ⊕ she was in the garage

2. She would come to check on him soon

3. Before they had married she had worked at a drive-in

4. Employees at the restaurant had taken turns doing different tasks

5. She had loved delivering meals to the cars in the lot

6. Getting to talk to the people in the cars had made her feel special

7. She had hated washing utensils at the sink in the back

8. Staring at the dishes in the sink of water had made her feel lonely

9. She always did all of the cooking when the family came

10. Out of politeness the family wouldn't allow her to wash up afterward

11. She nevertheless insisted on entertaining whoever was washing

12. She would keep chatting with the washers until the dishes were done

13. She was in the kitchen → she was entertaining washers

14. She was in the kitchen → she wasn't coming anytime soon

15. She was in the kitchen → she wasn't coming anytime soon

16. Before they had married she had been told she would never conceive

17. Her apartment hadn't had an air conditioner or electric fan

18. At night she had sat on the fire escape out the window for the breeze

19. She had raised her arms slightly ∨ she had dangled her legs over

20. While cooling off she had liked to imagine scenes of being a parent

21. Her favorite fantasy had been simply of doing crafts with children

22. For years she had believed those children would never exist

23. She kept craft supplies in a drawer in the dining room

24. She couldn't resist getting out the supplies when children were around

25. She could be happy indefinitely just making crafts with children

26. She was in the dining room → she was making crafts with children

27. She was in the dining room → she wasn't coming anytime soon

28. She was in the dining room → she wasn't coming anytime soon

29. Before they had married she had developed a habit of smoking

30. She had relished menthols ∧ she had savored cloves

31. For ashtrays she had taken castoffs from rummage sales

32. For matchbooks she had taken freebies from hotel lobbies

33. She had believed smoking would benefit her health

34. She found cigarettes revolting now

35. She was on a campaign to spread the word

36. Out of fear the family snuck into the garage to smoke during visits

37. She generally went out to reprimand whoever was smoking

38. She would keep harassing the smokers until the cigarettes were gone

39. She was in the garage → she was reprimanding smokers

40. She was in the garage → she wasn't coming anytime soon

41. She was in the garage → she wasn't coming anytime soon

42. ⊥

43. She wasn't coming anytime soon

∴ She wasn't coming anytime soon

He would have to go to her.

Wills gathered his strength, then trekked to the doorway at the end of the hallway, stopping once he got there. He had to place a hand on each side of the door frame to steady himself.

The lights were switched on, bathing the kitchen with incandescence. An array of photos were fixed to the fridge by magnets: a picture of him and his wife blowing up balloons for a birthday party; a picture of him and his wife splitting a slice of cake at a wedding reception; a picture of him and his wife raking leaves by the driveway, his wife holding up a snail by the shell, looking over at him with an expression of curiosity. The floor in the kitchen was made of tiles, which were generally less hazardous to traverse than the carpeting or the rug, unless water had been spilled, in which case some tiles would be safe and other tiles would be slippery, with no way of knowing. Video streamed across the tablet mounted on the counter, showing clips of floats covered in flowers, recaps of a parade. A mound of dirty dishes rose from the surface of the soapy water in the sink. Other tableware was piled on the counter next to the sink, crusted with hardened dressing, smeared with congealed gravy. A neon sponge lay abandoned near a deserted towel. His wife wasn't there.

A couple of people were making out: somebody with a moussed crewcut wearing a rumpled cardigan over a faded shirt, hunched over cross-legged on the counter; somebody with a broad forehead and a pointed chin wearing a lace dress, raised onto tiptoes on the floor. They kissed with urgency, heads craning back and forth for different angles, tongues sliding in and out. Their hands were pressed into the countertop, palms down, overlapping. Their eyes were shut.

"Should we find a closet?" the person in the dress smirked, reaching up to pinch a nipple of the other person through the fabric of the cardigan.

Peeking, the person in the cardigan began to respond, but then spotted him watching from the doorway. The person in the dress swiveled to look, saw him too. With an embarrassed expression, the person in the cardigan slipped down from the counter, picking up the sponge. The person in the dress grabbed the towel.

"We were just cleaning up," the person in the dress said, coughing, an indisputably false statement.

Wills stared, stunned to have discovered people nearly on the verge of mating in the exact place where he liked to wait when bread was toasting.

They got back to work, washing and drying the dishes, occasionally casting glances back over at him, as the pines swayed out the window over the sink.

Wills blinked, then shuffled into the kitchen, stepping carefully across the tiles in case of spills, crossing over to check the pantry.

The pantry was opposite the window, with a hinged glass door that swung both ways. The shelves were crammed with canned vegetables and boxed noodles. People rested against the shelves, arguing about something, voices muffled by the door. Each clutched a mug of steeping tea. Some were pinching the paper labels attached to the strings, tugging to make the tea bags bounce in the water. His wife wasn't in the pantry either.

Wills cracked the door open.

"You can't have both, you have to choose."

"I really hate when that happens."

"Here's the spectrum. At this end, you've got max safety and no privacy. At that end, you've got no safety but max privacy. The decision you have to make is how much power you want the government to have. This isn't hypothetical. This is reality. This is the situation we're actually in. Here's your choice. If you refuse to completely surrender your privacy, then terrorists will inevitably slip through. However. If you'll agree to completely surrender your privacy, then terrorists will have nowhere to hide. Now tell me what you choose."

"But drones are scary."

"But terrorists are scary."

"I think I've decided that I want something in-between."

"Yeah, so we'll still have some privacy."

"Well, then you'll also have some bombings."

"So you're saying that if we want our personal safety guaranteed, we'd not only have to let the police use drones, but we'd have to let the government put cameras everywhere, like even our homes."

"I could never agree to that."

"But why?"

"I'd really rather not have a bunch of dudes in suits sitting around watching me take a bath."

"Why's that?"

"I'm naked in there!"

"You let your doctor see you naked."

"But that's for health!"

"Getting beheaded in a shopping mall by a religious radical would also impact your health."

"I can't believe you said that."

"I also sing in the bath, that's probably the real reason."

"Fine, but if you won't let the government watch you in there, then that's where the terrorists will build bombs, is in their bathtubs, with their shower curtains drawn for privacy."

"This is making me really upset."

"There's nowhere you're as safe as a police state."

Everyone in the pantry turned to look at him as he pushed the door fully open.

"My wife?" Wills said.

Their expressions changed. Some appeared confused. Others appeared worried. They exchanged glances, nobody tugging at the tea bags anymore.

"Dad, what do you need?" asked someone wearing a diamond brooch.

Another reached out as if to take hold of him, but he jerked away, shuffling backward into the kitchen, letting the door swing shut. The people watched through the glass as he turned to leave. Nobody in there was going to tell him anything useful.

He crossed the rest of the kitchen—veering to avoid a dropped figurine, swerving to dodge a fallen rattle—heading for the doorway to the dining room.

Wills had taken the job shortly after the triplets were born. He'd never gone to grad school, he'd come home to help his parents try to save the bakery, but his parents had lost the business anyway. His parents both found work afterward—his father stocking shelves, his mother mopping floors—but that income alone wasn't enough to pay the bills. He not only needed to support his newborn children, but also had to help support his aging parents. He applied for anything in town with a salary, taking the first job he was offered, a sales position at an agricultural company he knew nothing about. The morning of his first day, his manager drove him out to see a goat pasture that the company contracted. The dawn was foggy. Dew slicked the grass. Goats were ruminating in the mist. Wills stood with his hands tucked in his pockets, listening with indifference initially but then with growing interest, as his manager explained the challenge ahead. Some analysts were calling it "the problem of the century": how to feed the exploding global population, which had already nearly doubled in his lifetime and was expected to double again before his lifetime was through. There were predictions of rampant famine, widespread riots, mass starvation, global conflicts. The planet's arable land wasn't going to increase; if anything the planet's arable land would decrease. To feed humanity—and avoid catastrophe—farmers would need to begin somehow producing quintuple the food per acre, a feat so improbable that success would be nothing short of a miracle. "How can you grow four stalks of corn in the same amount of space where you've only ever been able to grow one?" his manager said, slamming the gate back shut on the way out, head shaking in bafflement. "Get a cow to yield four times as much milk? Get a hen to lay four times as many eggs?" His manager climbed into the truck, calling, "It's like a goddamn riddle from some puzzle book." Wills frowned, reaching for the handle of the passenger door. He was still an atheist, but as he thought over the problem his manager had just described he was struck by such a powerful sense of destiny that a shiver passed over his skin, making his hairs raise. He'd been in a state of depression ever since giving up the grad school offer, but grad school seemed petty compared to this. He felt almost as if he'd been led back home for a reason. As a professor, the only good he would have provided was knowledge. But doing this, he could provide multiple goods: he'd be fighting to prevent famine and riots and starvation, maintaining social stability, bringing people happiness; meanwhile, he'd also be creating profit for the company, which would contribute to the overall economy, bringing people prosperity. By the time the truck swung back out onto the road, he'd gone from an apathetic hire to a company disciple.

The more he learned about the imminent disaster, the more his passion for the work grew. Although he later learned the company had been hesitant to hire somebody with a degree in philosophy, he rose quickly through the ranks, leaving the sales role behind for administration. His training in logic proved vital. Essentially, what the industry needed was increased efficiency, and he discovered he had a knack for looking at a process and reasoning out exactly how best to cut expenses and boost production. He took to wearing a beard, which he kept trimmed neat; he traded in his glasses for plastic contacts; his hairline began receding; his wash of freckles, though still present, was fading. He was famous for the habit of forgetting his suit jacket, hurrying off to appointments in just his shirtsleeves, with a tie flapping over his shoulder and his suspenders bulging at the chest. What he'd originally expected to be a temporary position ended up becoming a vocation. Wills believed in the work so deeply, he would have been willing to sacrifice just about anything to fulfill the mission, and that was ultimately what defined his adulthood: the clash between his devotion to the company and the demands of his family. He and his wife had bought a house, a bungalow with painted siding and a slate roof, the awning over the porch supported by broad pillars. The house was situated on a wide road with lofty trees, an idyllic development where kids on bicycles would often weave past while filling the neighborhood with the sound of laughter, and a bright layer of pollen would sometimes grit the surface of the cars in the driveways, and fireflies bobbed around the yards at night. His children were playful kids with piping voices who booed during cartoons whenever a supervillain streaked across the screen. His parents made a point of driving over most days after work, having finally found something to agree on, that being the importance of spending time with family. And there were moments during those early years in the development that filled him with a joy like he had never known: his children playing pool with his father in the rumpus room as he and his wife snacked on cashews at the bar and heckled both sides; his mother sewing finishing touches onto costumes in the laundry room as he and his wife stood brandishing brooms at the door to keep his children from trying to peek; a sunset breaking across the sky as his parents bickered on the swing on the porch and his children hula-hooped in the driveway and he and his wife spread woodchips across the flowerbeds in the yard.

If he had lived in a utopia, if there had been no disasters to avert or problems to solve, he would have wanted to spend every waking moment with his family. But he lived in what seemed to be on the brink of becoming a dystopia, and there were disasters to avert, and there were problems to solve. The work he was doing seemed worth any cost. There was something thrilling about taking part in such a monumental undertaking. The company was trying to save the world.

The company worked on the livestock side of agriculture, instead of with crops. The company owned the animals, which farmers were contracted to raise. This arrangement gave the company control over every aspect of animal production, so that any innovations could be implemented throughout the operations uniformly. And there were innovations in that era; there were miraculous breakthroughs in the industry. They discovered vitamins that allowed the animals to survive indoors indefinitely, thereby consolidating the operations, moving the livestock from scattered farms to condensed feedlots where record-breaking quantities of animals could be raised at once: hundreds of cattle, thousands of pigs, millions of chickens, in a single facility. Containing the livestock this way virtually neutralized any threat from predators, rendering coyotes irrelevant, weasels inconsequential, raccoons just nuisances with the garbage can. Furthermore, rather than needing a pasture for grazing, the animals could now be fed from troughs, subsisting on a carefully proportioned blend of vegetable by-products, bone meal, fatty tissues, offal, minerals, and chemical preservatives, a diet that not only was nutritionally optimal but was comparatively inexpensive. They used artificial lighting to manipulate the apparent length of day, compelling layer hens to produce eggs year-round; they dispensed arsenic to broiler chickens to grow fatter birds. They gave synthetic hormones to dairy cows, extending lactation periods for milk production; they administered steroids to beef cattle to grow larger beasts. They streamlined the process, installing conveyor belts for collecting eggs, fastening automated pumps for collecting milk. They utilized new technologies, transferring embryos between cows, inseminating sperm from bulls, so that cattle with desirable traits could be bred from just about any bovine with a womb. Even beyond these reproductive tweaks, minor modifications were discovered to offer major benefits, and they altered livestock accordingly, trimming back the beaks of the poultry, grinding down the teeth of the swine, stunting the buds of calves, cutting the horns from cattle, clipping claws and toes from fowl, docking tails from bovines and hogs, removing components that at this point for livestock were merely vestigial. They neutered any ruminant with testicles that wasn't going to be used for breeding. They devised effective ways of confining pregnant sows and inducing expectant cows. They developed efficient methods of culling rooster chicks. By dispensing daily regimens of antibiotics, they managed to eradicate illness from the animals nearly altogether.

And by eradicating illness and neutralizing predators and optimizing nutrition, losses of livestock were minimized, and the supply of animals actually managed to keep pace with the explosion of consumers. The livestock increased so drastically in size that new slaughterhouses had to be built for the animals entirely. With every breakthrough, a sense of achievement rushed through the industry, relief at having gained another edge in the war against famine. But by then the company had been absorbed by a corporation, and the corporation had been absorbed by a conglomerate, and the stakes just kept growing. Wills was making decisions with potential consequences for people across the globe. He'd never felt exhausted in college, not even after pulling all-nighters, but now he felt exhausted constantly, regardless of how much sleep he got. He wouldn't have wanted trivial work, but the pressure that came with doing important work could be crushing. Sunken pits darkened the skin beneath his eyes. He lived under the burden of his responsibilities: keeping the products flowing, to avoid the catastrophe of customers around the world being confronted with hunger; keeping the company profitable, to avoid the catastrophe of employees around the world being struck with unemployment. Having been born during the worst economic depression in living memory—having seen, as a child, the crowds of hungry waiting in line for free meals, the unemployed holding signs out on the street begging for jobs—the stakes weren't merely theoretical. He knew how quickly the good could be lost. His wife warned him that he was spending too much time at work, and he knew how much he was losing out on, but balancing his workload with his family was impossible. He'd manage to make a volleyball game, only to miss a science fair. He'd manage to make a dance recital, only to miss a forensics tournament. He just couldn't keep up, and every shift that he cut short meant the work fell that far behind, and he was already having to spend most weekends at the office by that point anyway. He'd come home to find the garbage container brimming with empty pizza boxes from a get-together he hadn't even known was going to happen; he'd comment on the new position of the chairs in the living room only to learn that the furniture had been rearranged weeks before. He noticed a dent in the bumper of the station wagon that his parents drove, and only then discovered that they had been rear-ended earlier that spring, which had made them late for a musical he'd had no idea his children had been any part of. They were becoming strangers to him, but given the choice between missing his family or failing humanity, the job was his priority. His children took his decision personally. He could toil for hours to scrub a chocolate stain from one of their favorite shirts, he could stay up until midnight helping finish one of their research papers, he could take them to a movie they had been begging to see, he could surprise them with homemade smoothies while they were cramming for exams, but that didn't matter. Any effort that was made seemed promptly forgotten, while any absence got permanently seared into memory. Wills sometimes glimpsed a look of anger when reaching over to give one of them a hug, or would glance up from washing the car in the driveway to see one of them watching him from the porch with an expression of spite. Once, over a dinner of steak and peas, he sat in shock as one of them burst into tears, sobbing at him that all he cared about was himself, squeaking out that he didn't love anything except his job, and then fleeing the dining room. That night he couldn't fall asleep, just lay there staring at the silhouette of the clock on the nightstand, thinking over the scene, until finally reaching over to switch off the buzzer a minute before the alarm was set to ring. He could still remember standing in the bathroom that morning, staring at himself in the mirror in the predawn light, looking into his eyes as if searching for some sign of what was going on in there. And then going into the garage and getting into the car and driving back to work.

And the country kept on invading other nations: dropping napalm on mountain villages, incinerating whoever happened to be there, leaving behind scorched corpses and survivors with deformed skin; gunning down random civilians in the streets of tropical harbors; plowing over trenches in the desert with armored bulldozers, burying enemy troops alive. And people on the home front seemed to be growing weary of the endless wars. By then he was spending most of his work-week at conferences out of state, and from the hotels where he stayed he would sometimes see protesters wearing peace signs march through the streets below wielding banners and billowing flags. In general his political leanings tended toward the right, but he could relate to the messages on the picket signs. The justifications for the wars had stopped making any sense to him at all. Any glamour the military had held for him as a child was gone.

His feelings about the protesters changed rather quickly, though, when the demonstrations turned on the agricultural industry. He was genuinely confused the first time he saw a picket sign referencing feedlots; he didn't understand what anyone could possibly have against being fed. As the movement began gaining momentum, however, he learned to expect environmentalists just about wherever he went.

The worst demonstration that he experienced personally was during a convention in Vegas. He and others from the industry stood at a bank of windows near the top of the escalators, watching the protesters gathered on the sidewalk outside the convention center. Signs bobbing in the crowd accused the industry of "atrocities"; others called for conference attendees to be "tried and hung as murderers"; others, less polite, said simply "fuck big ag." People dressed in cow costumes stood on milk crates hollering chants. Somebody burned an effigy of an executive. Leaving the convention center that afternoon, Wills felt compelled to lower his head as he passed through the crowd, which infuriated him, being forced to act as if he had something to feel ashamed of. A protester with cornrows and a tie-dye t-shirt moved to block his way. "Just read it man!" the protester begged, trying to press a floppy disk into his hands, but he shoved past toward a taxi waiting at the curb. Riding back to his hotel, he discovered the floppy had been slipped into a pocket of his trenchcoat. A strip of tape identified the contents of the disk as academic research on industrial farming. His blood was still racing from the encounter. He snapped the floppy disk in half and dropped the pieces into a garbage can in the lobby.

There was something disquieting about the fact that there were mobs of people out there who considered his work criminal. But the shifting attitudes toward the industry didn't truly bother him until the situation became personal. One of his children became a vegan, and then tried to hide it from him, claiming the change in diet was merely because of digestive issues, until his wife slipped the secret. When significant others came to visit during breaks from school, his children spoke the name of his company with obvious discomfort, as if he made a living by running sweatshops or scamming elderly investors. He overheard one of his children lie about his job altogether. If he complained about the demonstrations, tried to explain what the protesters didn't understand, he was given only polite nods, blank stares.

What finally made him snap was passing a billboard on the highway that referred to industrial farming as "the other holocaust." The comparison enraged him. He kept muttering the phrase to himself for the rest of the drive, spitting the words out like spoiled food. Even after parking his truck and going into his office, he couldn't stop brooding about the sign. He paced his office, drank a cone of water from the machine in the lounge, and then decided on a course of action. He'd been stationed at headquarters for decades; he hadn't visited the plants in years. He canceled his appointments for the week and arranged to tour some of the facilities.

He went looking for reassurance, a reminder of why he

did the work that he did. Instead, he discovered what efficient farming actually looked like when taken to the logical conclusion. He understood the rationales behind the methods, but there were details that emerged in practice that had been lacking in theory. He was baffled by the things he saw. Hogs confined to narrow crates, urine and feces left to fall through the slatted floor into a dank pit below, with the ammonia that rose from the waste so thick in the air that the fumes burned his eyes. Poultry crammed into barns so crowded that chickens had been trampled to death. Veal calves kept in stalls so cramped that any movement was near impossible, standing night and day on a cement floor crusted with mud and ice and frozen excrement, driven to inflict self-harm out of boredom. The tail of a lamb that had been removed by cutting off the circulation with a tight elastic band until the flesh had rotted and fallen to the ground, where his shoes suddenly brushed against it, scattering flies. Hens being starved to induce molting. Sows that had spent their entire lives in a near constant state of pregnancy being slaughtered as soon as barren. Cows that had spent their entire lives in a near constant state of pregnancy being slaughtered as soon as barren. Rooster chicks, inferior sources of meat and incapable of laying eggs, exterminated en masse by being knotted into plastic sacks to be suffocated to death, or being dropped onto electrified panels, or being funneled into gas chambers, or being tossed into grinders and ground up alive. Breasts so heavy that turkeys were incapable of flight. Udders so massive that cows struggled to walk. A swine fattened so rapidly that its legs had fractured under the weight. A chicken so overfed that its heart had failed from the strain of breathing. Animals that went their entire lives without once feeling the sun. Animals that went their entire lives without once feeling the wind. Animals, however, that had felt something, could plainly feel when alterations were being made, their beaks being scorched down, their horns being snapped off, their toes being lopped off, their teeth being grated down, their buttocks being cut off, their testicles being sawed off, with no anesthesia whatsoever. Admittedly, for anything with a nervous system, this was hell.

Wills found himself obsessing over the floppy disk he had left in the garbage can. When he returned to headquarters after that week of tours, he shut himself in his office, dialed onto the internet, and pored through scans of journal articles about industrial farming, searching for whatever he might have thrown away. He frankly didn't think that animals were entitled to rights, he thought human needs outweighed any concerns about animal suffering, but the studies he found online had implications even for humanity. The facilities produced so much excrement that even after saturating the fields with fertilizer there was always a surplus of manure that had to be stored at the operations in lagoons of feces, and fertilizer had on many occasions leaked from the fields, polluting nearby waterways, and manure had on many occasions spilled from the lagoons, contaminating the groundwater, and there were studies that linked the hormones in beef to significantly increased risks of breast cancer and prostate cancer and colon cancer in consumers, and there was evidence that employees working at the operations had a strong likelihood of developing both respiratory maladies and neurological diseases, and there was evidence that communities living in the vicinity of the feedlots had higher incidences of an assortment of ailments ranging from constant migraines to chronic phlegm, and between the manure contaminating the groundwater and the fertilizer polluting the waterways and the staggering amounts of water that industrial farms consumed there was now a looming water crisis that promised to be just as catastrophic as any food shortage, and glutting the livestock with antibiotics was causing bacteria to develop a resistance, threatening to render antibiotics, arguably the greatest medical advancement in history, completely ineffective, and meanwhile by some measures the methane discharged by livestock was contributing even more to global warming than gases released by automobiles, which would leave livestock to blame when the oceans turned to acid and entire cities vanished underwater and whatever cities remained onshore were ravaged by storms the like of which humanity had never seen. Essentially, the scientific consensus seemed to be that modern agricultural practices were wreaking absolute havoc on humanity, and had possibly fucked the species over beyond all hope of repair.

His coworkers didn't seem bothered by the issue—if anything, seemed offended, dismissing the protesters as a bunch of ungrateful hippies—but after that week of tours, he just couldn't concentrate on work. He sat in his office staring at the parking lot out the window blinds, sweating from the sunlight, letting the phone ring straight through to voicemail. He hadn't thought of his thesis from college in years, but he realized now how crude the system of ethics he'd proposed had been. A system that acknowledged only a single good was unreliable, but even a system that acknowledged multiple goods seemed inadequate. Because there were also chains of consequences, an action that had initially produced a good consequence might produce a bad consequence later, and the chains could build indefinitely. In college he had still been too young, hadn't yet witnessed how long an action could continue producing consequences. To decide whether an action was right or wrong, he thought, all the consequences needed to be taken into account: the immediate, the subsequent, the eventual, the ultimate. And in this specific case the consequences were becoming clear. What the industry had done had produced incredible good in the short term and in the long term had caused extraordinary harm. His parents were dead and buried. His children were grown and gone. He had devoted his career to an idea, sacrificed all that time with his family in an effort to help people, only to discover that the idea had been flawed all along, that the world was worse off than before.

Wills was standing just shy of the doorway to the dining room.

Something felt wrong with his shoes.

He glanced down.

1. One of his shoes had come untied

2. He must have stepped on the lace ∨ his steps must have loosened the lace

3. He always refused when she tried to convince him to wear different shoes

4. The aglets had chipped off ∧ the tips had frayed apart

5. The lace was flopped across the floor

6. He would try to tie it ∨ he would ask for help

7. He tried to tie it → he would bend over

8. He bent over → he might lose balance

9. He lost balance → he could fall down

10. He fell down → he risked getting hurt

11. When they were younger she had loved watching him do things

12. She had enjoyed watching him strain to lift sacks of gravel

13. She had enjoyed watching him stretch to reach the smoke detector

14. When going somewhere together she had always made him drive

15. She had liked to lean her head out the window as he drove

16. She had gazed over at him while squinting from the wind

17. She had enjoyed watching him maneuver the wheel

18. Now she didn't like him to lift up heavy things

19. Now she didn't like him to reach for elevated things

20. He wasn't supposed to drive

21. She would insist on helping him out of the car after she had parked

22. She pressed his trousers for him

23. She hung his shirts for him

24. She didn't like him doing things on his own anymore

25. She was always nervous he would get hurt somehow

26. She got especially anxious about him when family was around

27. She said the family believed he shouldn't be allowed to live at the ranch

28. She was scared the family would have him taken away to a home

29. She worried that the family was only looking for a reason

30. Him getting hurt today would distress her

31. Doing something would likely upset her → he shouldn't do it

32. He shouldn't risk getting hurt

33. He shouldn't risk getting hurt

34. He tried to tie it → he risked getting hurt

35. He shouldn't try to tie it

36. He shouldn't try to tie it

37. He asked for help → somebody would tie it

38. Recently something as simple as taking a shower could exhaust him

39. He was still tired from eating

40. The trek through the house had him winded

41. His arms were weary

42. His legs were aching

43. He was afraid to stop moving

44. He might be forced to sit by whoever came to tie it

45. He wouldn't have the energy to stand again

46. He would be stuck in a chair

47. Doing something would possibly strand him → he shouldn't do it
_____

48. He shouldn't get anybody to tie it

49. He shouldn't get anybody to tie it

50. He asked for help → somebody would tie it

51. He shouldn't ask for help

52. He shouldn't ask for help

53. ⊥

54. He would try to tie it ∨ he would ask for help ∨ he would just ignore it

∴ He would just ignore it

Wills stared at the lace, blinked, looked up, and kept going. The doors to the dining room were flung open.

He hadn't had the courage to quit the job, but he had lost all motivation after that tour of the facilities, and he had stopped making any genuine effort to perform. He didn't last at the company much longer. He got forced into retirement with a severance package that made his former salary look paltry.

He and his wife sold the place in Phoenix and bought a ranch up near Flagstaff, a one-story house in the mountains with a dilapidated stable and acres of bridle paths winding through the pines. The move-in coincided with a bitter windstorm that rattled the windows. He and his wife had settled on someplace in the mountains hoping for some peace. By then the country was at war again across the ocean, firing rockets at foreign tanks, shelling any building that was rumored to be harboring extremists, strafing any person who seemed even remotely suspicious from helicopters above, dropping cluster bombs indiscriminately across the countryside, massacring detainees periodically when the mood struck, carrying out revenge killings on civilians, torturing prisoners with sleep deprivation and stress positions and forced injections and deafening noise and extreme cold and severe heat and rectal feedings and strippings and hoodings and beatings and pissings and rapings while snapping pictures of the torture for fun. Wills was so sick of invasions, felt such guilt about paying taxes to a government that long ago had proven itself intent on using the revenue to slaughter as many foreigners as possible, that he couldn't even watch the broadcasts. The issue only reminded him of the fortune he'd earned by helping design an efficient system for murdering animals. He spent days sitting at the table in the dining room, watching the wind blow coils of snow from the drifts in the backyard, in anguish, as his wife moved through rooms in the background, untaping boxes, unpacking belongings. At night he lay awake staring at the streaks of moonlight on the ceiling, or at the dark when there were none. A week after moving in, he was dragging the garbage container down the driveway when that defect finally stopped his heart.

He woke in a hospital, hooked up to intravenous tubing and an electrocardiograph machine, in a bed across from a chair where his wife had fallen asleep. He probably should have been relieved when he realized he had been brought back to life, but instead he felt mildly bewildered. There would have been a logic to dying. He was finished working, he had devoted his career to trying to save the world and ultimately had caused mass destruction, and there was no undoing what he'd done. Even days after waking up, he still felt that way. Getting discharged rather than wheeled off to the morgue seemed like a mistake. There wasn't any reason for him to be alive. He should have died. Yet here he was, crossing the parking lot of the hospital, where the snow had melted to slush.

Riding back to the ranch, he and his wife stopped for shakes at a drive-thru, and as she leaned out the window to put in the order at the speaker, he sat there wondering what type of life he would have led if he thought like she did. Her mind had always mystified him. She had a brilliant intellect, could absorb foreign tongues in a flash, had grasped the principles of a combustion engine merely by glancing under a hood, had mastered the mechanics of a stock exchange without any formal study of economics, and yet contradictions didn't bother her in the slightest. She was an atheist who believed in heaven, a libertarian who supported universal healthcare, a pacifist who defended capital punishment, a romantic and a sentimentalist who regarded the grilled cheese sandwich as the epitome of beauty and considered holiday commercials to be sublime. She had no interest in discussions of logic. She decided what was true based on feelings. A philosophy of instinct and emotion. And she had known, she had warned him, that he would regret devoting so much time to work.

Sinking back into the seat, she commented on how cute he had looked in a hospital gown, then reached for the gearshift.

The cardiologist had told him his defect had been corrected, thanks to the surgery, and that his heart would last him "for years to come." Eventually, Wills came to terms with the fact that he couldn't change what he had done, and he set out simply to live out the time that he had left. To have as little effect on the world as possible. To experience. To observe. His head went bald; his freckles vanished entirely; he let his beard grow wild, into matted clumps that his wife claimed were handsome, which somehow never turned gray. And though he was never able to bridge the distance that had formed between him and his children, he was startled to discover that the relationship between him and his wife was undergoing a revolutionary transformation. A marriage that for decades had been based primarily on sexual attraction and a mutual interest in raising a family was gradually evolving an intimacy that had never been there before. The clinging devotion of childhood outcasts turned best friends, of committed spouses, of grateful mates, of nestled companions who could wake up late, eat a brunch of fried eggs and fig yogurt and buttered toast with rhubarb jam, read the newspaper, drink some espresso, make love on the rug in the hallway, shower, and spend the rest of the day hiking the bridle paths in the forest, touring a winery, shopping for snowshoes, and feasting on a platter of homemade nachos heaped with cheddar and beans and tomatoes and peppers in the light of a noir film playing across the television. As if all along she had only been waiting for him to take the time to fall in love with her. Although he didn't believe he deserved it, those decades after retiring were the most peaceful era of his life—but his memories from those later years were hazy, nowhere near as crisp as his memories from earlier years. A meager set of ordinary moments that he hadn't forgotten when there were so many that he had. Chewing a shortbread cookie in the pantry, his shoes pocked with wet leaves. A child in a light blue sweatshirt unexpectedly pushing a puppy into his arms. Grandchildren in baggy nylon jackets chasing a flock of swallows out of the stable with a roar, and afterward sprawling on the dirt in some sunbeams, gawking at him with expressions of awe as he topped off the mower with gas. His wife gathering fallen pine needles from a boulder, and rubbing the needles between her hands, and then after clapping the needles away holding out her palms for him to sniff. His wife swaying with a martini, barefoot but still wearing a cocktail dress from a fundraiser gala, rambling with excitement about how a certain expressionist painting made her feel. His wife sitting in a bathrobe on the chair in the office, her face caked with a mask of clay, her finger raised in the air for silence, gazing out the window with a wary glint to her eyes as gunshots echoed somewhere out in the fog. Folding emerald wrapping paper around a present at the counter in the kitchen as his wife insisted that he was doing it wrong and rejected any claim that he knew what he was doing and grew increasingly irritated and finally just pushed him aside to wrap the gift herself. Blinking awake from a nap on a warm dusty afternoon and discovering that his wife had woken before him and was lying there studying him with a smile. Riding a chairlift during a group outing to the local ski resort, feeling the seat sway as wind lashed the chairlift, watching the shadow of the chairlift ghosting along the slopes below as the retired banker next to him offered a monologue on the role of the country in global affairs, remarking with a sense of finality, "This was our century."

Wills was ashamed of how much he'd shrunk, ashamed of how his skin had withered, ashamed of how hunched his spine was, ashamed of how his ears drooped and ashamed of how his jaw sagged, ashamed of the sour odor his body emitted that didn't seem to wash off, ashamed he had to wear glasses with lenses so thick that his eyes appeared magnified, ashamed he had to wear a plastic hearing aid in his ears that some-times chirped and startled everybody, but all of that shame, all of it, was nothing compared to how he felt about the de-mentia. He couldn't remember when he began noticing the symptoms, which itself was probably a symptom. He would go out to the garage, only to forget what he needed, forget why he even needed it, standing there at the workbench wracking his brain until in a state of utter exasperation he would finally be forced to go back into the house empty-handed. He would lose track of where he had put certain belongings, wasted en-tire afternoons looking for stamps or scissors. Scheduling ap-pointments, he confused which order the days came in, would have to fumble for the calendar. Poring through a magazine, he would sometimes get a nagging feeling that he had already read the articles before. Doing the finances, he botched basic computations, became frustrated by the inscrutable complex-ity of the buttons on the calculator. He began to withdraw, avoided talking whenever possible, afraid that he might lose track of what he had been saying midway through the sen-tence, or that he might suddenly forget a word he needed to complete the thought. He hid the symptoms the best that he could for years—from everyone—until ultimately his shame was overcome by his panic that the symptoms were worsening. Sitting in his underwear on a paper sheet on an exam table, he finally confessed what was happening, hoping his physi-cian knew of a drug that could halt the process. His physician reached for a clipboard. "Sometimes the mind goes before the body," his physician said gently, and then offered to prescribe a medication that, his physician explained, would only delay the inevitable. Wills glanced away, staring at a chart hanging on the wall, feeling the utter terror that he hadn't felt when he had almost died. A raw grief. At losing, after so long, the faculty of reason. The ability to speak that language he had learned as a child.

But as his mind deteriorated, his marriage only grew stronger. The sense of intimacy, of clinging devotion, took on a frantic quality. No matter how unpredictable his behavior got, no matter how frequent his episodes became, no matter how many times he hurled the remote at the television in an inexplicable fit of frustration, or glazed over at a tub overflowing with water, or wandered away from a stove with lit burners, or came to among a mess of smashed vases and ripped curtains and broken lamps, his wife hid the worst from the family, insisting she wanted him there, at home, with her. In lucid moments, when he thought about his life, he thought that marrying his wife was the only indisputably good thing he had ever done.

Wills slipped into the dining room.

There were photographs everywhere even in there, a portrait of him and his wife on the wall above the credenza, snapshots of him and his wife and various children arranged in paint-chipped frames within the china cabinet, an album on a seat cushion flipped open to pictures from a vacation, anywhere they had ever lived his wife had filled their rooms with photographs, so that wherever he looked the past was always present. The dining room was lit by the chandelier above the table. The napkins had been crumpled, but hadn't yet been discarded; the placemats had been stacked, but hadn't yet been cleared. A citrusy smell rose from the tabletop, the scent of whatever cleaning solution had been used to wipe off spatters and crumbs. Fluorescent noisemakers lay scattered across the floor. Beyond the windows, the blizzard raged. Desperation seized hold of him as he realized his wife wasn't in there.

People were perched in the chairs, children in skirts and pullovers, an assortment of ages, sipping from glasses of punch while chatting back and forth. The bowl, which sat at the head of the table, was made of glass that had been pressed with symbols of berries and vines. Sherbet floated in the punch.

"Like isn't there something weird about being sentient?"

"What's sentient mean?"

"Conscious or whatever."

"Something that's really been on my mind a lot lately is, you know how we came from monkeys? And how we were the first intelligent species? Well, what if some other family of animal had evolved intelligence first? Because the race must have been pretty close, right? I mean, pigs and dolphins are really smart. Chickens can count, and stuff like bears and crows and elephants can all use tools. Bees communicate by dancing, and squid talk with colors, and whales sing."

"Ah, that ice cream is giving me a total brain freeze!"

"So, what, instead of smart monkeys there would have been smart chickens or something?"

"Yeah, but think about how different the world would have been! Like what if the first intelligent species had evolved from bears? I mean, they've got families and stuff, but they don't run around in troops like monkeys do, and plus what would a society even look like that had been built by animals who hibernate? Or what if the first intelligent species had evolved from elephants? They aren't omnivores like monkeys are, they only eat like grass and bark, and anyway wouldn't a society run by animals that had a mating season be pretty weird?"

"The reason that I keep laughing is, imagine a world where everybody had the personality of a squid."

"Or like a pig."

"I mean, of all the animals, why us?"

"You're kinda making me wish that monkeys hadn't won."

"That's what I can't stop thinking about is, would the world have been better or worse if we hadn't? What if we weren't the best ones? What if we were the worst ones?"

Somebody tipped a scoop of punch into a glass, heavy on the sherbet, and then slipped the ladle back into the bowl.

"I heard some kids on the bus say that evolution isn't real."

"Well, those kids are idiots."

"If nothing else, monkeys have the best sense of humor, so our civilization must at least be the funniest."

Wills interrupted.

"Where did my wife go?" he asked, enunciating through clenched teeth.

The children turned to look at him. Somebody wearing barrettes froze in the midst of a sip. Somebody with spectacles and braces had paused reaching for the ladle, eyebrows up, mouth agape. A clock ticked on the wall. Nobody responded, the children didn't say a word, and his back hurt, and his feet hurt, his skin was bristling with rage, all he wanted was some solitude, and there wasn't a room in the house that wasn't occupied, these people hadn't left him anywhere, and still nobody was telling him where his wife was, and he'd had enough of being ignored.

Wills shuffled closer to the table and pointed at the children with a jab.

"Where is she dammit?" he barked.

The children stared at him with frightened expressions.

He grabbed a child by the shirt, squeezing the collar in his fists.

"You tell me where the hell she is," he growled, giving the child a rough shake, and when the child still didn't respond he slapped the child across the face.

The child burst into tears.

Wills had raised a hand to slap the child again, but the tears startled him. He realized he'd done something wrong. Staring at the child, he released the collar, backing away, and as he did the lace of his shoe caught under the treads and he lost his balance, reached out to steady himself, and instead of grabbing hold of the table grabbed the rim of the punch bowl, which flipped under his weight. The punch hit the floor with a smack, the bowl shattered on impact, and the sudden noises made him jerk, sending his heart racing. Bumping past an empty chair, he fled the dining room, glancing back at the horrified children and the spilled punch and the broken bowl. As he stumbled into the garage, the chill struck him in a blast, the garage door was up, snow had blown in from the driveway, each stall was occupied by a car, the lamp over the workbench was off, the light on the ceiling was dark, and nobody was smoking, the garage was empty, his wife wasn't out there either. He turned from the driveway and hurried past the workbench, fumbling open the door to the backyard, trying to get away, afraid there would be consequences for what he'd done.

The blizzard had stopped. He struggled across the backyard, his shoes sporadically breaking through the layer of ice between the fresh powder and the older snow, sending him plunging to the ground with his arms suddenly buried past the wrists, until he fought back up again, his fingers burning from the cold. A grit of frost crusted the knees of his khakis. When he reached the edge of the pines, he stopped, breathing heavily, and glanced back toward the ranch.

The window frames lining the rear of the house gave him a view of the various scenes in the rooms indoors: the television shining across the people gathered in the living room; periodic bursts of fire from the children crouched in the tub in the bathroom; the gleam of the phones in the bedroom making silhouettes of the people sitting atop the comforter; a shadow flapping across the walls above the teenagers lit by the lamps in the office; the bright lights illuminating the people washing dishes in the kitchen and the people sipping drinks in the pantry beyond; under the glow of the chandelier in the dining room, the children at the table pointing down at the mess on the floor, explaining something to the crowd of people who had come to investigate the noise. And even from out there he couldn't see his wife anywhere.

Wills suddenly became aware of a suspicion that had been building in him ever since he had gotten out of his chair: that she was dead, that she had been dead for years, and that he had already forgotten that she was dead so many times now that people had given up reminding him.

The theorem stunned him, because he could see the rationale behind the idea, understood exactly how everyone might have decided that would be the right thing to do. His knees wavered, and wind rushed out from the pines behind him, cutting straight through his flannel, making him shiver. Powder blown from the pines floated down around him, leaving faint indentations scattered across the surface of the snow. All the frustration he'd felt about not being able to find her was gone, replaced by the panic that gripped him at the thought of never seeing her again. Getting agitated was making him confused, which only agitated him more, which only confused him more, until everything was muddled. He didn't want the smells of her cooking and her lotion and her shoes to fade from the house, he didn't want mail to pile up on the table instead of her forcing him to listen as she read the messages on cards from family aloud, he didn't want the carton of margarine in the refrigerator to have burned crumbs from toast mixed in that nobody had nagged him to clean out, he didn't want the bed to have an empty side, to have to sleep next to a blank space, tonight or ever, and he wasn't sure anymore whether she had been there during the meal at all, and if she was gone, and if he kept forgetting, then how many times had he already had to relive that moment of first knowing she was dead, like now?

Overwhelmed, he glanced up at the sky, trying to make sense of what he knew.

1. The ape family had produced a sapient species

2. A calendar was never sartorial $\rightarrow$

3. $\qquad\qquad$ $\rightarrow$ a magazine was always multicursal

4. The ring on his finger was a wedding band

5. The watch on his wrist was a stem-winder

6. Politicians were logicidal $\leftrightarrow$ politicians were logicidal

7. Apples $\vee$ oranges

8. His children had once spoken an idioglossia

9. His umwelt no longer included a sense of taste

10. The moon was dark

11. The stars were out

12. The air was so cold that when inhaling his nostrils burned

13. Language was being used to segregate

14. Something was made $\therefore$ money $\rightarrow$ something $\therefore$ was not art

15. Terrorists were planning even now to execute innocent people but

16. The government was spying even now on innocent people but

17. Yes was a confirmation $\wedge$ no was a negation $\wedge$ mu unasked the question

18. Mood affected initial impressions $\leftrightarrow$

19.   ↔ subliminal perceptions influenced behavior

20. In certain lights the snow glittered very

21. At night icicles seemed especially

22. His lungs were so warm that the air turned to mist when exhaling

23. Chemical weapons could be odorless

24. The bees were vanishing ∧

25.   ∧ The flowers were disappearing ∧

26.   ∧ The glaciers were melting away ∧

27.   ∧ The lakes were drying up

28. There was a zeitgeist

29.   → Humanity needed to get off-planet →

30. ¬ (Was stillness) ∨ was stillness

31. Bird sang birdsong

32. ∀ keyholes ∃ unbecoming

33. ¬ (Was plenum ∧ ¬ ¬ ¬ (were infrared ∨ were ultraviolet ∨ ¬ ¬ (was collop

34. Teetotum hendiadys gossypiboma orrery coffle syzygy pelf

35. Without ⊥ ⊕ ⊤ how could ⊕ ⊥ ⊕ ⊤ ⊕ ⊥ until ⊕

∴ Pudding?

He stood there in the snow, consciousness whirling with irrelevant axioms and incomplete propositions, an ancient organism in the mountains of a terrestrial planet drifting in orbit around a main-sequence star. It was a new year. He was almost a century old.

A woman in a neon beanie and a billowing peacoat was staring at him from the door to the garage, holding a newspaper tucked into a fluorescent bag, looking furious.

"Bud, what are you doing out here without a jacket?" the woman demanded.

He hesitated. Then he tried to explain that he didn't know, that he'd forgotten what he was even looking for, but before he could speak the woman was already crossing the backyard. Keys jangled in the pockets of her peacoat. Her boots broke straight through the ice. Grizzled wisps of brittle hair hung from the rim of her beanie. She wasn't wearing gloves. When she got to him, she took hold of him, gripping him tight.

The woman led him back toward the house. But before they reached the door, they stopped, because she had noticed that he was crying. She asked what was wrong. She wasn't angry anymore. She sounded worried.

"Bud, what's the matter?" the woman said again.

He looked at her, wiped his face, and smiled.

"Everything's going to be all right," he said, because, at that moment, that was what he honestly believed.

Acknowledgments

<salute>To the writers who mentored me as a student: Tony Earley, Lorraine Lopez, Jill McCorkle, Nancy Reisman, Heather Sellers, and Danzy Senna.</salute>

Gratitude^{Prostration} to Vanderbilt University, the Fulbright Commission, the MacDowell Colony, the Whiting Foundation, the Ucross Foundation, the Ragdale Foundation, Vermont Studio Center, Blue Mountain Center, Virginia Center for the Creative Arts, Prairie Center of the Arts, and the Djerassi Resident Artists Program, who fed and sheltered me throughout this project.

A hearty cheer {*formula*} in tribute to the editors and readers at *Conjunctions, Hayden's Ferry Review, Kenyon Review, New England Review, The Missouri Review,* and *The Southern Review,* with special thanks to Dana Diehl, Gary Garrison, Allegra Hyde, Carolyn Kuebler, David Lynn, Micaela Morrissette, Bradford Morrow, Emily Nemens, and Evelyn Somers, who supported these stories and the earlier prototypes.

Praise is due → hail Jenessa Abrams, Anders Carlson-Wee, Marie-Helene Bertino, and Beth Jacobs, whose feedback was crucial to revising this collection; hail Sarah Burnes, a brilliant adviser, a generous friend, and the world's preeminent literary agent; hail Michael Griffith, James Long, Neal Novak, and the rest of the crew at Louisiana State University Press, who worked spiritedly and tirelessly to accommodate all of the special formatting and symbols in this book.